The Obsessed Hero and the Villainous Family's Daughter

악역가문의 막내딸에게 남주가 집착하면

OU HEUNG

EDITIO

PUBLISHING

The Obsessed Hero and the Villainous Family's Daughter
OU HEUNG

Cover Illustration by MUMONG

악역가문의 막내딸에게 남주가 집착하면 by Ou Heung

Copyright © 2020 Ou Heung
Cover Illustration Rights © 2022 MUMONG
All rights reserved.

This English edition was published by Editio Publishing LLC in 2023
by exclusive contract with Kyobo Book Centre Co. Ltd.

ISBN 978-1-959742-18-0 (Print)
Produced in the United States of America

editiopublishing.com

EDITIO
PUBLISHING

The Obsessed Hero and the Villainous Family's Daughter

Contents

Chapter Thirty-One 1

Chapter Thirty-Two 12

Chapter Thirty-Three 23

Chapter Thirty-Four 34

Chapter Thirty-Five 44

Chapter Thirty-Six 56

Chapter Thirty-Seven 68

Chapter Thirty-Eight 76

Chapter Thirty-Nine 88

Chapter Forty 98

Chapter Forty-One 109

Chapter Forty-Two 118

Chapter Forty-Three 129

Chapter Forty-Four 140

Chapter Forty-Five 151

Chapter Forty-Six 162

Chapter Forty-Seven 172

Chapter Forty-Eight 184

Chapter Forty-Nine 192

Chapter Fifty 203

Chapter Fifty-One 213

Chapter Fifty-Two 223

Chapter Fifty-Three 234

Chapter Fifty-Four 243

Chapter Fifty-Five 253

Chapter Fifty-Six 265

Chapter Fifty-Seven 275

Chapter Fifty-Eight 285

Chapter Fifty-Nine 294

Chapter Sixty 304

CHAPTER
THIRTY-ONE

"By the way, do you even know how to drive a carriage, My Lady?"

Of course, I... don't know how to drive a carriage. I know how to ride a horse, though.

"Not at all."

I smiled brightly and stuffed Jane into the carriage. She struggled, trying to resist, so I ended up having to kick her lightly in the rear.

It was nice not wearing a dress for once. A dress revealed your status too easily, gave away too much. Your status restricted what you could do, where, when, and with whom... *A noble lady in a dress, driving a carriage? Impossible. A noble lady shooting the breeze with her maid? The maid would get in trouble.*

Everything I had done today was things I wasn't allowed to do as a noble. Seeing how different things were with just an outfit change was fun. I liked the freedom it entailed.

At first, when I was reborn, I was thankful to be reborn as a noble, but it soon felt like I had given up my freedom in exchange for a warm place to sleep and a full stomach.

However, others might point fingers and say I'm being ungrateful.

I leaped onto the driver's seat and cracked the whip.

Neigh! The horse released a long whinny and started galloping. A loud crash sounded—something broke inside the carriage. Hoping it wasn't Jane's head that had just burst, I drove on.

Two knights stood guard in front of Rodrigo's quarters. They were in high spirits, ready to use all their might to block anyone who hadn't been preapproved from entering.

Inside, Rodrigo sat with Gunther and Devlon. A heavy atmosphere weighed down the room. The three men glared at a map spread out on a table, their arms crossed as they contemplated.

"I expect we will have one week." Gunther broke the silence.

The week he was referring to was the amount of time he expected them to last in this war before they had to raise a white flag.

"Sir Gunther is overestimating things. We should pack our bags this very night if there is to be an ambush." Devlon spoke in his usual, overly solemn tone.

Rodrigo didn't reply. His thoughts were in chaos.

"There is a way." Gunther glanced at Devlon, who shook his head as if to discourage him from continuing, but Gunther was determined.

Since Gunther had clearly prepared something, Rodrigo tore his gaze away from the map and looked at Gunther.

He prompted him, "Go ahead."

"We can surrender."

Rodrigo exhaled a huff of laughter before lowering his head again.

"Think about it, Your Grace," Gunther rushed on. "Emperor Thereo has thrown us into the fire. What difference does it make whether we win or lose?"

Gunther was right. Emperor Thereo had sent Rodrigo to war so he would die, or at least return completely wrecked, with his spirit broken. The emperor might even be humming delightedly as he considers the many ways he could command Rodrigo to make up for the loss. However, if he won...

Emperor Thereo would pressure Rodrigo, claiming that he was ready to rebel. The easiest way out of all this would be not to return, but that had never even been an option.

"What if I use magic?"

"Your Grace!"

"Absolutely not!"

Gunther and Devlon trembled in agitation. Rodrigo's magic

was still unstable. If Emperor Thereo found out that he could wield magic, he would pounce on him immediately. He could never stand to let such a threat go free. The emperor as a potential enemy versus him becoming a definite enemy were different matters entirely.

"There's just no other way."

For the first time, Rodrigo felt cornered on the battlefield. He could not overcome it alone, through sheer strength or force of will. He had already survived so much in his life, but this... *Is this how it ends? With nothing to do but pass the time?*

"Your Grace, Your Grace!" the knights guarding the door outside called urgently.

"What is it?"

They had ordered them not to interrupt unless there was an ambush. Gunther rose from his seat and opened the door.

"Uh... hm?" Gunther mumbled in surprise at the door, peering outside.

"What is it?" Rodrigo followed Gunther to the door to find out what the problem was.

What had Gunther at a loss for words? Rodrigo looked outside, and then he froze.

"E-Estella?"

Looking filthy and on the verge of death, Estella announced, "I'm starving."

"Ah, we nearly died."

I only regained my strength after gulping down a full bowl of hot soup.

"Does anyone else know you are here?"

I nodded. Not only did they know, but my whole family was on its way to find me and bring me home. I had nearly been caught on my way here. Fortunately, my family hadn't expected me to dress up as Jane's carriage driver, so we had been able to get out from under their very noses.

"How did you come all this way? Had you planned this after I left for battle?" Rodrigo held out a handkerchief.

The slightly stained cloth, very unlike him, made me pity him. He was always well-dressed, clean, and tidy. He was described in the novel as looking refined even when speaking roughly.

Thinking about how he had had to use the same wrinkled old handkerchief for months did not sit right with me.

"I apologize. The situation here is not very good."

He apologized as I fiddled with his handkerchief instead of wiping my mouth with it. He seemed to be blaming himself for offering me something less than perfect.

"I came here knowing that the situation wasn't good," I

told him.

I wiped my mouth as if to emphasize my point and wiped my hands on the other side of his handkerchief as well. Rodrigo's gaze rested on my hands.

"This place is dangerous. You must leave immediately. Actually, why did you come here?"

He gave me a look that showed he had no idea why I could be there. He seemed flustered, unable to decide what to say first, and was throwing questions in my direction to get a sense of what was happening.

Calmly, I looked at him and smiled.

"I came to tell you how to end this war quickly."

He couldn't hide his bewilderment.

"Nothing."

"I've failed again today."

"I couldn't find her."

Count Kartina exhaled a string of sighs at his children's disappointing reports. Three days. Three whole days had passed since they had chased after Estella through the portal. Count Kartina was so worried that something terrible might happen to Estella, who had grown up so sheltered, that he was on the verge of going insane.

"What if she found him already?" Ada, who had been eyeing her father warily, muttered.

"What? No way. We chased after her immediately. Estella isn't that fast."

"I agree. She's not familiar with this area, either."

Ayla and Kalen could not see past the image of their naive baby sister that Estella had cultivated. The same went for the rest of her family. To them, Estella was someone who would starve to death if she was ever stranded on a mountain because she couldn't even catch a rabbit and who, if she came across a ruffian, would give him every coin she had and more. She knew basic fighting techniques but had never so much as flicked anyone on the forehead. None of them could comprehend how she could think to find Rodrigo all on her own. Her family members were worried sick.

"At least Jane is with her."

That much was a relief.

"Do you think Estella might have been attacked by ruffians in this area?" Kalen muttered but quickly shut his mouth.

The inn they had completely rented out was filled with murderous intent. A few knights lost their grip on their swords, and the birds that had been sitting by the window flew away.

"Take down anybody suspicious in this area. If anyone has seen even a glimpse of Estella, bring them here."

Why hadn't they considered that the further you went from the capital, the fewer guards there were? And that meant there were more gangs and thieves here. Why hadn't it occurred to them that the beautiful, lovely, adorable, and precious Estella would be a prime target for these evildoers?

The sound of teeth grinding and jaws clenching filled the room. They stretched out their necks and picked up their respective weapons. It was late at night, a time that suited them very well. They slipped into the darkness, blending in like shadows, and began to comb through each surrounding neighborhood. They hunted gang after gang, questioning dozens of even slightly suspicious individuals, searching for *someone* who might have seen Estella.

Rodrigo considered Estella's words.

"I came to tell you how to end this war quickly."

Curious, he frowned at her. How could she know such a thing? Still, judging by her confident smile, she surely had a plan.

However, they couldn't continue their conversation. Another message arrived from the imperial palace.

It hadn't been long since he had received the refusal for backup, so he wondered what it could be this time. Rodrigo had everyone leave. Estella could have stayed, but she left him alone anyway. She said she would look around the campsite, and Rodrigo didn't stop her. He knew this message wouldn't contain any good news. And he was right.

"Hurry."

That was it. A short letter implying that he should lose the war and return to the capital with his head bowed as soon as possible.

Rodrigo sighed. Though Gunther and Devlon were against it, he had no choice but to use his magic. Rodrigo flexed his hand, feeling the stretch of the tendons and a tingling sensation up through his wrist. A bright blue light flickered over his palm.

"May I come in?"

A small head poked past the tent flap to peek inside. Startled, Rodrigo hurriedly relaxed his hand. Still, the light must have lingered because Estella knew right away.

"Did you use magic?"

Rodrigo hesitated for a moment before nodding.

"Can you use it freely now?" Estella walked around the tent as if inspecting it as she asked Rodrigo.

He leaned against the table and stared at her. At times, she would speak as if she knew him extremely well. And most of the things she said were correct. Everything from small, insignificant details to important events from his life.

Just now, for example. Her question implied that she knew he had been having difficulty using his magic. And that was a very well-guarded secret.

Who on earth was Estella?

"Can you use it freely now?"

I surprised myself when this question slipped out. I was acting far too much like I knew everything. I knew that he was in pain whenever he used magic, but that wasn't enough to justify my knowledge of a fact he had been keeping secret.

However, it was too late now. I couldn't take back what I had just said, so I studied his reaction carefully as I walked around his tent. Rodrigo spent a long moment staring at me as if trying to look inside my mind, but he didn't say much about it.

"Let us continue our conversation."

It was finally time for me to talk about why I was here. I dragged a chair over and sat in front of him and then gestured for him to do the same. It was uncomfortable to stare up at him since I had to throw my head back. He followed my lead without complaint. I then calmly explained my plan.

A kidnapping ploy.

As he listened to my plan, his expression hardened. And when I was done talking, he yelled, "Absolutely not!"

His eyes flamed.

CHAPTER
THIRTY-TWO

Why is he mad?

I wasn't used to seeing Rodrigo taking deep breaths as he tried to suppress his anger. He was usually a calm person. His anger threshold was very high. Truthfully, he rarely became angry about anything. If he wasted his energy on getting annoyed at every little thing, he would have to be furious all the time because of all the unfortunate things happening in his life.

"Is there something wrong with my plan?"

"Yes. A lot."

He clarified that he didn't want to talk about this subject any longer as he took a swig from his flask. His anger stung a bit, and my pride hurt. I thought I had come up with a pretty good plan. I never thought it would get rejected as soon as I suggested it.

"What exactly is wrong with my plan?" I asked sharply.

He exhaled a sigh and took another swig from his flask.

"Because you will be in danger."

What? I didn't know what to say, so I kept my mouth shut.

I am a Kartina. I was hiding my abilities, but I was skilled enough to take on Kalen, Ada, or Ayla, each on their own without any trouble.

In danger? Me? The Kartinas would exterminate the Velokis before anything could happen to me. Before I even used my own abilities, I mean. Even if something went wrong, I would have no trouble taking care of myself—but Rodrigo didn't know that, I suppose.

I told him, "There's no need to worry about me. I am strong."

"So are the Velokis. Especially Franz."

Franz? Who's that? Oh, does he mean the young prince that he helped out? I remembered briefly reading about him in the novel. There was one paragraph about Rodrigo's association with the Veloki Kingdom. Because of this connection, Veloki later helped Rodrigo. The fact that they had become enemies at war on Emperor Thereo's whim when they should have been helping each other left a bad taste in my mouth.

However, there was no use fretting over it now. They were at war, and Rodrigo had to win no matter what.

"You have to win, though. The emperor refused to send backup, didn't he? Your soldiers are already exhausted, and morale is low. There is no other option."

Rodrigo furrowed his eyebrows. He pursed his lips and then opened them, seeming like he had much say. Instead, he kept his mouth shut. All that was left between us was silence. He must have emptied his drink because Rodrigo just kept fidgeting with his flask. I could sense how frustrated he was, and it frustrated me too.

The air was so thick that it was hard to breathe. This was not what I expected when I entered the portal at the Kartina Manor. I had imagined that Rodrigo would welcome me and that he would rejoice at the solution I brought.

"Damn it," he muttered. Then, he added, "I apologize."

The rough words didn't affect me. I'd become used to cursing while running around after the Kartinas to try and mitigate the damage they caused.

"I was talking to myself. Give me a chance, Estella. I will win this war."

"But how?" *You don't even have a plan.*

"I did not want to resort to this, but I plan on rattling the king."

Oh my, maybe he does have a plan. My eyes glinted. What did he have up his sleeve? In the end, I had finished reading this novel because I liked Rodrigo as a character and was entertained by the way he solved tricky situations exactly like this one.

"Why don't you leave it to me and go back home? I do not think I can take on the Kartinas as well."

His expression was strange. He seemed worried and annoyed, even a bit bitter.

"The Kartinas will need some time to find me," I reassured. "So why don't you tell me your plan and—"

"General! General!"

Before I could finish my sentence, it suddenly became noisy outside the tent. Rodrigo grimaced as he rose to his feet.

"What is it?"

"Well... Count Kartina has arrived."

A bolt of ice in my stomach. *What? How? How did they find me so quickly?*

Rodrigo's jaw gaped open and then closed into a sharp frown.

"Estella!"

The five Kartinas ran to me and began to search me for injuries. They grabbed at me, running their hands over my arms, inspecting me for any scrape or bruise. Both Kalen and Count Stefan had tears streaming down their faces, and my eyes welled up at their obvious devotion.

However, Ada and Ayla immediately drew their swords and raised them to Rodrigo's chin. Gunther and Devlon lunged forward to stop them, but Rodrigo waved them away.

"This is outrageous. Even for the Kartinas..." Gunther and Devlon mumbled.

After ensuring I wasn't hurt, Kalen turned to Rodrigo and screamed, "You bastard! How dare you kidnap our Estella!"

"No, Kalen, that's not—" My words became lost in everyone's chaos.

Rodrigo, though he could have countered the insults thrown his way, simply listened. His eyebrows twitched as if bothered, but otherwise, he remained completely calm.

You were practically trembling with anger when I suggested I play hostage, I thought.

Kalen stalked closer and closer to Rodrigo. He glared at Rodrigo so hard that the whites of his eyes showed as he huffed and puffed.

"If anything had happened to Estella, I would have killed you!"

"If that had happened, I would have died long before you could kill me."

It was the first thing Rodrigo had said since the Kartinas had barged in and caused a scene. There was a force behind his low, calm voice that caught everyone's attention, even amid all the shouting.

"Wh-what?"

"Are you done?"

Rodrigo brushed a hand over his face before pushing aside Ada and Ayla's blades. Then, he slowly stepped closer and halted before Count Stefan, who was wiping his tears.

"I think it's my turn to get angry now."

He glanced over at me. *Is he asking for my permission?*

"Go ahead, Rodrigo."

I was certain that he wouldn't be as rude as the Kartinas were, so I nodded.

"I cannot understand how you could let Estella come to such a dangerous place on her own," he said clearly.

Stefan's face reddened. It was normal to become flustered when someone pointed out the mistake you were acutely aware of.

Uh oh.

"Was it not you who brought her here, Sir Rodrigo?" Stefan clenched his teeth. His jaw was locked so tightly that he could hardly pronounce his words.

"What kind of foolish man would bring his fiancée to a place like this?"

Stefan exploded at the word, screeching, "I will not allow this union!"

"I'm going to win this war, Count."

It was the first time Rodrigo had referred to Stefan without the title. Among nobles, titles trumped everything else. Stefan twitched, clearly agitated, but he didn't correct Rodrigo.

"And then I will get the emperor's approval for our marriage."

Rewarding someone who had won a war that nobody expected to be won with approval for marriage was nothing. After all, most royals would give their daughters away for marriage as a reward.

Stefan clenched his fists.

"It appears that you have already lost this war."

Stefan had concluded that Rodrigo was going to lose. I shook my head. I couldn't let Rodrigo lose this war. I had to do something so that the Kartinas wouldn't have a choice but to help him now that they were already here.

Rodrigo had said that he had a plan, but it was always better to have more forces on the battlefield, especially when those forces were highly skilled. Even if just the five Kartinas present participated, it would change things for the better.

"I want to go to war too!"

My hand shot in the air to catch their attention. The Kartinas, who had been crowding around Rodrigo, all turned to look at me. The tent went so quiet that you could even hear an ant's footsteps.

Kalen was the first one to break the silence. He stepped over to me and grabbed me by the arms.

"What did you just say, Estella?"

"I said I wanted to lend my strength to the empire's forces."

"Estella! Your heart is as noble—no, much nobler and more precious than that of a hero wanting to save the empire, but— Estella, the battlefield is far too dangerous for you!"

Ada and Ayla, who had come up behind Kalen, nodded. Now I was the one surrounded by the Kartinas.

"But everyone is risking their lives for the emp—"

"Estella, let me tell you about war..."

And thus began their attempt to change my mind. Their description of war was as fantastical as something straight out of *The Lord of the Rings*.

"There are headless horsemen out there."

"The horses they ride are those that have crawled out of their graves too."

"There are men with swords for arms."

What a mess.

Gunther and Devlon gave each other exasperated yet amused glances.

Oh man... this is really embarrassing.

Even Rodrigo, who had been on edge, was now pinching the bridge of his nose with an exasperated smile of his own.

"I really want to win this war!" I exclaimed, clenching my hands into fists in determination.

"Why, Estella?" Kalen looked at me as if he just couldn't understand.

I took a deep breath before responding firmly. "Our family has always been loyal to the emperor! We've always been at the forefront when the empire was in danger!"

Technically, it was more accurate to say that our family worked in the shadows. Still.

"I want to be a Kartina that everyone can be proud of."

I looked at both Hela and Stefan, my eyes glistening with unshed tears. I couldn't expect them to be convinced by logic. When it came to me, the Kartinas were entirely irrational.

"Estella, you... have such a valiant heart." Hela wrapped her arms around me. "I had no idea. I thought you had left us because you were so in love with Rodrigo."

It was true that I had left for Rodrigo's sake, but I kept my mouth shut, figuring it would be better to let Hela misunderstand the situation.

"Then we will participate in your stead."

Ada and Ayla put their hands on each side of my shoulders. "What?"

When I turned my head, still enveloped in Hela's embrace, I came face to face with Ada's solemn expression.

"We can't allow you to go somewhere so dangerous, Estella. I'm sure Sir Rodrigo feels the same way."

When she looked over at him, Rodrigo nodded.

"But..."

"We just have to win, right? We'll be enough."

"If we want this to end quickly, I guess I will have to step up as well."

Stefan cracked his knuckles.

I smiled inwardly. *Yes!* It would have been better if I could have brought hundreds of soldiers, but the Kartinas counted for a hundred soldiers each. My heart swelled with confidence.

"Ada, Ayla, Kalen. Also, Father and Mother. You are all so amazing."

Their expressions melted like whipped cream on a hot summer's day at my praise.

And so, they all went out to war the next day. I sat on a chair inside the war tent, having done my best to act as though I was determined to join them and letting them talk me down.

Jane approached me. A shadow fell over my head. I was slumped down with my chin on the table as I looked over at her.

"I got scolded so badly!" Jane pouted.

I remembered belatedly that Stefan and Hela had called Jane out last night.

"Sorry."

I had decided against defending her because I didn't want to stir the hornet's nest and had remained inside the tent.

Then I had fallen asleep before she had returned and hadn't been able to console her.

I had been busy seeing everyone off to war in the morning after that. Everyone had wanted to hold my hands, embrace me, and stare dolefully into my eyes, so it had taken quite a while. I was quick to offer an apology, unlike most masters.

"I would like a raise."

"Sure."

"I want a crate of those vegetables from Sir Rodrigo's greenhouse delivered to my home every month."

Wow, she's really getting her money's worth.

"All right."

"And one more thing."

"There's more?"

I sat up, my eyes wide.

CHAPTER
THIRTY-THREE

"Why? Do you think it's too much?"

I did, but I shook my head.

"No. I know how much you're sacrificing for my sake."

I also knew that she could take care of her many family members thanks to this job. Jane pulled out a chair and sat across from me.

"It's about Sir Gunther."

"Hm?"

"Can you look into his background?"

Whenever she mentioned him, Jane's eyelashes seemed to tremble.

Oh? I narrowed my eyes at her, but she turned her head to avoid my gaze. This made me certain. A romance had finally come to Jane as well.

"Don't worry, Jane."

I was determined to make Jane's love come true even though my own love couldn't come true for the sake of humanity and the world.

"That makes me worry even more," Jane said, though she

clearly didn't mean it.

"Oh, so you're saying you trust me? Thank you." I took a deep breath and smiled at her.

However, then our thoughts drifted to what was already at hand.

Quietly, I asked her, "Do you think the battlefield will be chaotic?"

Inside the quiet tent, Jane and I each thought of those we cared for on the battlefield. There was no chance that Rodrigo would die since he was the main character, but he could still get hurt. Worried, I bit my lip and tried not to think about it.

"Estellaaa!"

At sundown, everyone who had gone to battle returned. Battles in this age tended to follow a natural rhythm. Some small ambushes occurred at night. However, when it came to large-scale wars at the border like this, a fairly strict timeframe was followed.

A battle would be declared in the morning, and then it would take place in a specified location. The location would inch toward the other's territory depending on who had been victorious the previous day. If one side was decisively stronger than the other, they could make it to the enemy's headquarters in only a day. Still, when both sides were practically equal, as was the case now, the fight could stretch months on end, with the battles occurring back and forth between the territories like a two-step dance.

However, they had found victory today.

"Do you know how great I was today? I started by beheading the general and laying waste to the place," Kalen chattered excitedly.

Then Ada followed. "Estella, when I swung my whip at the horses, dozens of soldiers just collapsed like dominoes, and—"

"Stop exaggerating," scolded Ayla. "I used some poison. They fainted right away, so I used them as stepping stones to get to their commander and cut off his head. Would you like to see, Estella?"

"No, that's all right, Ayla."

I could picture it clearly. The rule-breaking Kartinas suddenly appearing amidst an army of rule-following soldiers and triggering utter chaos. I took a moment of silence for everyone who had been killed at the hands of the Kartinas.

Still, where was Rodrigo?

"Estella!"

As I was about to look for him, Stefan and Hela arrived. I ran toward them and threw myself into their open arms. Hela and Stefan squeezed me tightly.

"Were you scared?"

"This place is safe, so I had no reason to be. You aren't hurt, are you?"

I scanned Stefan and Hela. My siblings couldn't avoid my hawk-eyed gaze, either. Nobody was hurt. Unlike their children, Hela and Stefan did not immediately boast about their accomplishments. However, judging by their smug looks, I could tell they had achieved a great deal today and were itching to tell me all about it. Still, I wanted to enure Rodrigo was safe first.

"Hold on, Mother."

I gently removed Hela's hand that was holding mine. Hela's eyes narrowed. She sneaked an arm around my waist, having realized that I was looking for Rodrigo.

"He is taking care of the injured soldiers."

My eyes widened. Hela smiled and released me from her grip.

"I killed more!"

"Nuh-uh! I killed at least a hundred."

"A hundred? I stopped counting after about one hundred and fifty."

My siblings squabbled over who had gotten the most kills.

"Don't just stand there chatting. Go inside."

As Stefan attempted to break up the fight, I hurried toward

the tents designated for the injured.

Unlike where the other soldiers were, the atmosphere here was glum. It even felt like the colors were dimmer here, all blacks and grays. Splashes of red were like beacons in the darkened fields. The other soldiers were celebrating because this had been the biggest victory since the war began. However, this noise was full of groans punctuated with shouts of pain.

This is what war is really like.

"Lady Estella, it would be best for you not to enter."

Gunther, covered in blood, stood in my way.

Remembering Jane, I took a moment to assess whether Gunther had been injured, looking him up and down. Fortunately, he seemed fine. A sudden cold rushed through me as I wondered whether it was appropriate to use the word "fortunately" and be relieved. Here, where people had just died. Not too far away, a soldier who had lost a leg lay on the ground. His face contorted in pain, but there was nothing I could do. Nearby, another soldier had blood streaming down his face. I took a slow breath, feeling pathetic for being relieved that someone I knew was safe when so many others weren't.

"Please, go back. You shouldn't have to see this, My Lady," Gunther insisted stoically.

He seemed to have misunderstood the reason behind my hardened expression.

"No. I'm here to see Rodrigo."

"He is busy at the moment."

I tried to take another step, but Gunther blocked me. I raised an eyebrow. Gunther wasn't usually like this. Normally, he tried his best not to interact with me. It was strange that he not only stood in my way but was also having a fairly long conversation with me. Why was he doing this?

I told him, "Rodrigo must have commanded you not to let me in."

His large muscles twitched.

"I know what you are worried about, so step aside."

I reached out a hand toward Gunther. He seemed startled by my proximity and stepped aside. Rodrigo might have commanded him to stop me, but I was sure he wouldn't dare use force. I took another deep, slow breath and set my jaw before continuing to look for Rodrigo.

It didn't take long. I saw Devlon entering a tent with a bucket of hot water. Barring specific circumstances, Devlon was always by Rodrigo's side. I followed him.

"G-general... My family... My sister..."

I paused at the voice coming from inside the tent.

"Bono, you should take care of your family yourself. There's no need to ask me. Hang in there, Bono. It'll be all right."

I knew why he was saying those things. Someone was dying. He was comforting a dying soldier, reminding him, panicked in the face of death, why he had to survive.

"It hurts s-so much. So much..."

His sobs crashed into my chest, breaking my heart. I wondered how Rodrigo must feel as the leader of his soldiers when even I had to resist the urge to cover my ears. More painful sobs—it was unbearable.

"When you get back, what do you want to do first, Bono?" Rodrigo's voice was steady.

"My sister... My sister is getting married soon. I want to walk her down the aisle..." His voice trailed off, as if he was gradually losing consciousness.

I held my breath.

"That's right, Bono. You'll return and walk your sister down the aisle. So she is getting married soon? I will buy her a wedding dress. So Bono, just... Bono!"

His quiet voice suddenly boomed, and my held breath burst out painfully. I knew what had just happened. Bono was dead. I had no idea who he was, but I knew that he didn't deserve to die on the cold ground, away from his family. I lowered my head and mourned his death with a moment of silence.

"He is gone, Your Grace," Devlon announced.

There was some rustling, and Rodrigo emerged from the tent. His hair and clothes were disheveled. Dark circles framed his eyes, which widened at the sight of me.

"Oh... I came to check if you were all right," I said. I pursed my lips, unsure what could be said at such a moment.

"I am just fine, as you can see," he said.

He forced a smile as he raised his arms. He was apparently uninjured and thus fine, but also not fine at all. Sure, he was all right physically, but he looked as though his spirit had been torn to shreds by a dozen blades. I didn't know what to say to comfort him.

"Shall we go for a walk?"

All I could do, all I could think of at that moment, was to allow him a brief respite from this place.

"Yes, let's do that."

Rodrigo stepped beside me.

"General!"

The soldiers called to him and saluted him as we passed. Rodrigo pleasantly greeted all of them, even the lowest-ranked soldiers who took care of the horses.

"I apologize," he said as I stood awkwardly beside him, pausing our walk every few steps to acknowledge the soldiers in return.

"There's no need to apologize," I said. "It's nice."

As he nodded at each and every soldier, I thought about the household staff at Kartina Manor. *Do I know all their names?* I suddenly remembered Rodrigo going completely berserk in the latter half of the novel. He had stopped talking even to Devlon and Gunther by then. *Had he ever really looked at anyone warmly, really seeing them?*

"Estella?"

Like he was now.

"Yes, Rodrigo?"

"Were you frightened? At the medical tent earlier..."

"No! I've seen plenty of injured people."

Wherever the Kartinas went, they would leave behind all kinds of injured people. For that reason, I had also learned first aid.

Truthfully, the Kartinas haven't been as active these days. It seemed they didn't have enough time to torment people because they were so preoccupied with spying on Rodrigo and me. Maybe my decision to announce my intent to marry him had been a good one all around.

Rodrigo and I walked in silence. We passed the tents and reached the lake. When selecting a campsite, being near water was important since it was necessary for washing and cooking.

The location Rodrigo had selected for this camp was perfect. I admired the strategy in the choice, recognizing his natural leadership. We looked out on a path snaking between overgrown thickets, firm ground, and a wide lake with clear water.

"Shall we rest for a moment?" Rodrigo asked.

I nodded. Then I flopped down onto the soft grass without another thought.

"Estella?"

When I looked up at his surprised tone, I saw that he had been in the middle of taking off his coat.

"You shouldn't sit on the ground like that."

He dusted his coat before placing it on the ground next to me. I didn't object and shuffled over to sit on his coat instead.

"I should have offered you a handkerchief to sit on, but I don't have one."

He seemed really obsessed with handkerchiefs ever since we first met. *What a gentleman,* I thought as I looked out onto the lake with him silently. It seemed silly to worry about what I was sitting on when people were dying, but his concern for my well-being, especially in these trying times, made me feel special.

On the lake before us, whenever the water's surface rippled, a long silver fish burst into the air. The breeze was cool, and the darkening sky picturesque with languid, trailing clouds.

"Estella."

He spoke up first.

"I apologize for showing you such a shameful side of me."

"What?" I responded, as if I had no idea what he was talking about.

"Losing countless battles, having to get help from your family, failing to protect my own soldiers..."

Self-deprecation didn't suit him.

"None of that is your fault," I told him how I honestly felt, my brows furrowing in frustration. "None of the things that had happened to you were your fault."

His gaze wavered. Just like the lake's rippling surface when a fish broke through to jump into the air.

His face inched closer to mine. I knew what that meant. I closed my eyes, my cheeks feeling warm, my heart fluttering in anticipation. Our lips were about to touch—

"General! General! Deserters!" a voice called out to him.

CHAPTER
THIRTY-FOUR

Rodrigo and I hurried back to the tents, where Devlon gave a report. Rodrigo's face darkened.

"Who is it?"

"A small unit of troops has fled."

"Find them. Capture every single one of them."

What's happening? Why would they flee when they just had a huge victory? I stood there, mutely contemplating this.

"Go back to your tent, Estella."

Rodrigo turned to look at me. I wanted to stay, to help somehow, but I would probably make things harder for him if I insisted on staying. I nodded and headed toward my tent.

"My Lady! Where have you been? Young master Kalen has been looking for you."

Jane was clearly upset. I consoled her by telling her about having seen Gunther, and she calmed down enough to start cleaning again.

"Sit down, Jane."

Jane stopped patting down my sheets and stepped closer. She had been muttering about the lack of proper bedding. Soft blankets were an extravagance you couldn't expect to find at a war camp. However, considering Jane was just concerned for me, I didn't point this out.

"What is it, My Lady?"

"If you were a soldier, when would you choose to desert?"

"When my death was certain," she replied straightforwardly.

"Right? That's what I think too. Isn't it strange to run away when victory is just a few days away?"

"No, My Lady, you misunderstood me. I wasn't talking about winning or losing a war. My life being in danger is the crux of the issue."

Hm? I considered Jane's words. She was saying that it had to do with your death becoming certain, regardless of the war's outcome.

Oh! A new realization struck me. The soldiers who ran away had glimpsed at the horrors of death for the first time today. Or their built-up anxieties about death had been triggered. *What can the reason be?*

"My Lady, if that's all, I'll start cleaning," Jane said, ensuring I was done asking questions.

I simply nodded, thinking then of what Kalen, Ada, and Ayla had told me of their achievements. What they had bragged about would have been terrifying for the enemy but also for our soldiers.

I stood up from my seat.

"I'll be back."

"Where are you going?"

"To do some damage control."

"My Lady!"

I left Jane, who was calling me desperately and started running.

I found Rodrigo leaning back in his seat with his eyes closed.

"Are you asleep?" I whispered quietly, not wanting to wake him if he really was asleep.

He looked exhausted.

"No." Rodrigo straightened slowly, blinking blearily.

Yes, you were. There were telltale signs that indicated someone had been asleep. Rodrigo stretched his arms above his head. A button must've popped off of his shirt because I could see his taut muscles. Suddenly feeling warm, I looked away.

"About the deserters. What will you do with them?"

"I will deal with them as military law dictates."

"You mean you'll have them killed?"

Rodrigo paused while sipping water. He looked at me for a long moment.

"You seem to have many interests. Are you knowledgeable

about military law?"

I hadn't studied it or anything. It was just something that seemed to happen a lot in fantasy novels, so I just assumed the punishment would be the same.

"Not particularly."

"You are correct. Their leader must die. And the rest will be branded on their foreheads and treated as slaves on the battlefield for the rest of their lives."

"Is that really necessary?"

It was cruel. I couldn't stop myself from asking.

"It is."

There was something unfamiliar about this side of Rodrigo. I knew deserters had to be punished. Still, even for desertion, I couldn't help thinking this punishment was too harsh.

"Think about it, Rodrigo. They aren't much different from Bono."

As soon as I said it, I knew it was a mistake. I shouldn't have mentioned the name of a soldier who died after fighting valiantly on the battlefield before him. Rodrigo's calm expression shattered.

"Estella," he said lowly and sharply. "Do not compare them with Bono." He met my gaze, his expression like stone. "I think you should leave now."

He stood and walked to a map hanging on the tent wall.

This was the first time Rodrigo had turned his back on me. I knew it was my fault, but it still hurt.

"Rodrigo, this is my fault. If you mean to punish them, you might as well punish me too."

"What do you mean?"

He turned his head to look at me, so I stood up from my seat and faced him. The table and chairs between us only created more distance.

"The Kartinas joined the battle because of me, and those soldiers were terrified by them."

Thinking about it now, I wonder whether the Kartinas had even bothered to differentiate between enemy and ally soldiers. They would've, of course, been targeting the enemy. Still, there might have been casualties on our side in their wake.

"You are reaching. Even if that were true, the Kartinas were instrumental in our victory today."

He seemed determined to deal with the deserters by the book. He wouldn't change his mind no matter what I said. That steel gaze would not give in, so I had no choice but to give up trying to convince him. He seemed so far away from me.

"It would be best for you to leave, Estella," Rodrigo said.

His words were like knives in my heart.

"Let's go home."

I had accepted Rodrigo's command and immediately returned to the tent where my family members were gathered. I took up my small pack of belongings.

"Good idea, Estella! Let's go."

"What about the war?"

Unlike the rest of my excited family, Hela was calm as she asked me this.

"I imagine they will negotiate now that there's been such a decisive victory. I'm sure they'll get a declaration of surrender soon enough."

Hela seemed convinced by my reasoning as she stopped questioning me.

"If we leave now, we should be able to arrive at the nearest portal by evening," Stefan said.

Going back home was much easier than finding the war camp. We didn't say goodbye to Rodrigo.

Two months had passed since we left the camp. Three months since the war began. It had turned into a war of attrition. Against my expectations, the Veloki Kingdom did not surrender and continued fighting. Part of me was proud of Rodrigo for continuing to fight when he was short on supplies and soldiers. I was aware of the situation, but I couldn't just step up to help him. He hadn't sent a single message. And I hadn't contacted him, either.

I was only able to hear news about him whenever I met Detheus. After we returned from the war, Stefan began to visit the imperial palace frequently. And every time he went, he asked me to join him.

I didn't want to go—I knew what Stefan was after. Still, I couldn't stay away as soon as I had met Detheus by chance and heard the news of the war from him. Detheus begged me to sit in front of him and spent hours bragging about himself until I looked unmistakably bored, at which point he would give me bits of news from the war as if appeasing a petulant child with candy.

"There will soon be a new king in Veloki, Lady Estella," he whispered as if it was some great secret.

"Pardon?"

"It has been decided that someone loyal to the empire should take the throne."

The Veloki Kingdom was not a vassal state of the empire. However, they had been subservient to the empire and had thus earned the right to choose their own king.

And they plan on ignoring their sovereignty?

"When that happens, there will be a coronation with a

grand banquet to celebrate it, so why don't we go together?"

I forced a smile. Detheus's hand was inching closer to mine on the table. I lowered my hand from the table, away from his, before I answered.

"Wouldn't we have to pass the battlefield? I do not wish to go somewhere so dangerous."

"Oh, the war? It'll be over soon."

What?

"The pope has made a move, you see." He laughed.

What is he talking about?

I returned home and sat at my desk. I recalled the pope's face, whom I had met at the ball the other day. Nathaniel had a youthful face with lips so red they could almost be described as provocative.

He had a large role to play, but I just couldn't remember the details. Then again, it had already been seventeen years since I arrived in this world. It made sense that my memory of the novel had become hazy. The pope had done something important during this war, I knew. Still, what? Uneasiness crept through me. I couldn't ignore it, but I couldn't remember.

I wish I could talk to Rodrigo about this.

Unfortunately, after the incident with the deserters, things had become awkward between us, and we hadn't contacted each other still. According to Detheus, Rodrigo was keeping himself busy.

What should I do?

I soon found the answer.

"Jane!"

"Yes, My Lady?"

It wasn't long after I had rung the bell that Jane came in.

I said, "Help me get ready to go out."

"Where are you going?"

The carriage headed toward a dense forest in the north of the capital. We were on our way to the papal court. Though most cities had temples in their centers, the center of the capital was occupied by the imperial palace. The papal court was located behind the palace on top of a tall mountain, and the building was twice as tall as the imperial palace. Indeed, when you stood in front of it, you came to realize just how tiny you were, just how insignificant a human life was. It was such a natural response that the architecture seemed deliberate.

"Welcome, Lady Estella."

I ran into Nathaniel just as he exited the building, seemingly by chance. He recognized me immediately.

"Good day, Your Holiness. It has been a while." I greeted him as elegantly as possible.

He gave me a benevolent smile. Seeing such a grandfatherly smile on such a young face seemed strange.

"What brings you here?"

"I came to see you, Your Holiness." I wasn't one to beat around the bush.

"Oh? What an honor. But unfortunately, I was just on my way out. How about you make an appointment next time if that is all right?" he said politely.

I recalled what Detheus had said. He said that Nathaniel would be heading to the battlefront soon. Perhaps he was on his way. I needed to find out whether Nathaniel would help Rodrigo or cast him into a pit of despair—before he left.

"Is that so? Would it be possible for me to join you on your way out? That would be more than enough time."

Nathaniel narrowed his eyes, evidently suspicious of my insistence. He peered into my eyes as if looking straight into my soul, his lips forming a thin line.

Don't say no, don't say no. I pleaded inwardly.

Nathaniel's red lips parted as if he had finally made a decision.

CHAPTER
THIRTY-FIVE

"Let us go together."

I breathed a sigh, relieved. Nathaniel didn't reject my suggestion. He escorted me to his carriage and had me enter first. As I sat down, he climbed inside and sat across from me. He looked at me, but we didn't say anything for a while.

"The weather is quite nice."

Nathaniel opened the window, and I glanced outside. The sky was a clear blue. The forest's thick scent wafted inside. I took a deep breath. I had been anxious before meeting Nathaniel, but I was calm now.

"Why did you come to see me, Lady Estella?" He looked me directly in the eye.

His golden eyes, symbolic of the pope, were fascinating. It was something about your eye color changing when you received a holy revelation.

"I heard you were going to the battlefront."

"Oh yes, you are correct."

"Might there be anything the Kartinas could help you with?"

Nathaniel smiled brightly.

"How kind of you, Lady Estella." He added a blessing.

"I only wish to fulfill my duties as a noble." I had no intention of befriending him. I kept my tone cold on purpose.

"You are being modest. But I have no need for your help this time."

That was not the answer I expected. I had heard the temple was always short on money, which was why they liked nobles. Nobles brought in cash. It had become commonplace for the rank of the priest giving the blessings to change according to the amount of money offered. Whenever any special occasions were held at the temple, the priests asked for money outright.

He's going to the battlefront and doesn't need money? With the horses and rations for his entourage, there would be plenty of need for money.

"I suppose you won't be able to take much with you since we are in the middle of a war." I needed more information.

Nothing.

I tried again, "With so many injured men, you must need a lot of priests capable of using holy magic."

He simply smiled at my words without responding.

I gritted my teeth and tried again.

"Prince Detheus said that you are going to end the war. As a citizen of the empire, I look forward to it."

His smile faltered for a moment. I would have missed it

had I not been staring at him. What caused that twitch, that tiniest downturn of his red lips?

I decided to test it by mentioning each element separately.

I said, "Prince Detheus really is delightful. And he cares deeply for our people."

"I see."

The words left a sour taste in my mouth, having to praise Detheus to gauge the pope's response. Unfortunately, Nathaniel didn't react.

I didn't give up.

I said, "More importantly, you are amazing for intending to end the war that has been going on for three months already. You must have a great plan."

Aha!

The corners of Nathaniel's lips stiffened. His smile remained plastered on his face like a mask, but I could tell now that he tended to press his lips together more tightly when he tried to smile more widely.

"It has nothing to do with my own strength. It is all god's plan."

He turned to look outside the window as he said this. It clearly indicated that he no longer wanted to speak to me.

I wonder what it is.

He was hiding something. It would be weird for him to tell

me everything when this was only our second encounter. Still, it was also strange for him to be so on guard when I had been praising him this whole time.

"Prince Detheus seems to have found favor with you. I suppose Sir Erhart is... quite a dangerous man," he said.

We seemed to be nearing his destination because he dragged the thick holy book he had placed next to him onto his lap.

"Sir Erhart is dangerous?" I asked.

Instead of a response, he smiled.

"If you have any lingering feelings for him, I suggest you get rid of them. If you need any help, please come see me."

He blathered something incomprehensible before opening the door and hopping off the carriage as it slowed.

"Take Lady Estella to the Kartina Manor," he shouted to the driver before disappearing down a small alleyway.

"Your Holiness!" I raised my voice as I called after him, but he didn't look back.

I slumped back onto my seat. His last words bothered me.

"Aaargh!"

Screams of pain tormented the otherwise quiet forest, silencing the birds and echoing through the hollows between the trees. The horrific cries were coming from Gunther. Blood gushed from his thigh like a fountain.

"Gunther!"

Rodrigo, who had been riding ahead, turned back and began to stop the bleeding.

"We got hit. It was a web."

Devlon looked around and discovered the reason behind Gunther's injury.

"A witch's web?"

"Yes."

It had been two months since they had infiltrated the Veloki Kingdom to cause chaos from within. Soon, a new king would rise to the throne. Emperor Thereo remained unaware, but Rodrigo had been behind this development.

Franz, who had ascended as the king of Veloki, had discovered forces planning to use this war as an excuse to oust him. Rodrigo had contacted Franz covertly and suggested a plan that would ensure both he and Franz would survive.

Rodrigo planned for Franz to step down from the throne after admitting defeat. The new king would announce that Veloki would become a vassal state of the empire. Then, they would stir up a rebellion, and Rodrigo would go for the king's head.

Since the enemy's king would be dead, the war would not be considered lost. Rodrigo was planning to weasel his way out of Emperor Thereo's trap by neither winning nor losing this war. Franz agreed wholeheartedly.

He was aware that the situation in his kingdom was not going well and had received a report that those planning a rebellion were frequently meeting up with agents of the empire. With Rodrigo's help, Franz was slowly preparing to step down as king.

Rodrigo was on his way back to the battlefield after wrapping things up. For two whole months, he had been spending his time as a general on the battlefield during the day and as Franz's strategist at night, which meant that he hadn't had any time to write to Estella.

Finally, he no longer needed to be Franz's strategist. He had been planning to write to her in peace that night, but then they had come across a witch's web.

"I-it won't stop bleeding!" Devlon exclaimed, having taken over for Rodrigo in trying to stop the blood from pouring out.

Gunther writhed in pain, making it hard to put continuous pressure on his wound.

"Where's the nearest temple?"

A witch's web was hexed. Only holy magic by a priest could get rid of a hex.

"Well..." Devlon trailed off, sounding hesitant.

Rodrigo remembered that they were still inside the Veloki

Kingdom. The empire and Veloki worshipped different gods. If they were to receive treatment from a priest here, they would be considered heretics. However, there was no other way to save Gunther.

"We're moving. Now."

As soon as he made his decision, Rodrigo used his magic. He stopped the bleeding and dulled Gunther's pain with healing magic. As the pain receded, Gunther closed his eyes and fell asleep. Rodrigo staggered.

"Your Grace!" Devlon tried to steady him with bloody hands, but Rodrigo stopped him.

"It's fine. Let's go."

Devlon draped Gunther over his shoulders. They headed toward the nearest Veloki temple.

"What?"

Jane looked solemn as she delivered the news that was spreading around the imperial palace.

"Rodrigo? A heretic?"

"Yes. The rumor is that it is why the pope has gone to the battlefield."

Oh, that explains why he said that. That Rodrigo was dangerous, and I needed to watch out.

"There's no way. He doesn't believe in the god of the empire, but that means he doesn't believe in any other gods, either."

He was an atheist. That alone was a great sin. However, in any case, it meant that he would never serve the Veloki kingdom's god. Jane shrugged.

"He might have wavered since the war isn't ending."

"Jane!"

When I called her name sharply to reprimand her, Jane avoided my gaze, turning her head away.

I need to help him. Still, I couldn't think of how.

I asked Jane, "How far has this rumor spread?"

I had to plan for the worst-case scenario, so I would plan with the assumption that the pope had gone to the battlefield for a witch hunt.

"Only a few people know about it, even in the imperial palace."

It had really been worth taking Jane with me whenever I had gone to the palace, seeing that she had managed to find out such a heavily guarded rumor.

"I have to go to the Erhart Manor."

When I arrived at Erhart Manor, Augus was loading things into a carriage.

"Greetings, Lady Estella. I was going to visit the Kartina Manor soon to see you."

"It's nice to see you, Augus. Have you been well?"

We exchanged the usual formalities.

"Yes, I was. But I apologize for your presents being so delayed."

"Presents?"

August looked pleased as he gestured toward the three carriages.

"What is all that?"

"These are presents that His Grace Rodrigo ordered to be sent to you before he went to war. In that carriage are specialties from the Luwens Kingdom. This one contains precious fabric and gemstones... Oh! And I have recruited a designer as well, Eve Saint Laura! It was so difficult to recruit her because she is affiliated with the Kartina family. Only when I told her that the dresses would be going to you, My Lady, did she agree."

Augus looked very pleased with himself.

"Wait a minute."

He prepared all these presents before going to the war where he may die?

"There's more. He decided on everything before he left, but I had a hard time getting my hands on everything. I shall send them to you as they arrive," Augus continued even after I had interrupted him.

I couldn't understand Rodrigo. This was too much, even for show. And it was even stranger that a man who had meticulously prepared all of these presents didn't write to me for two whole months.

"I'll take a look at these gifts later. I have something to tell you, Augus."

Augus, who had been serving the Erharts for a long time, was a wise man. He was also incredibly loyal and served Rodrigo until the novel's end. It was beyond valuable to have a trustworthy person in a situation where no one else could be trusted.

"Is this true?"

Augus's wrinkles became more pronounced once he had heard what I had to say.

"I apologize. It is not that I do not trust you, Lady Estella..." he said, apparently thinking that it had been rude of him to question me.

I told him it was fine as I raised my teacup. Augus seemed to need some time to digest the information. I was sure that he, too, was afraid of the repercussions of what I had just told him.

A heretic? From one of the founding families of the empire?

Not only would he lose his title, but he would also be criticized by the empire's citizens. It would be a huge blow to the Erharts, who valued their reputation above all.

"What can we do?" Augus asked.

I really didn't know, either, which was why I was here.

But one thing is certain.

"We must save Rodrigo."

We need to save him.

"We need to confirm this rumor first," Augus said.

We needed to confirm whether Rodrigo had really resorted to joining forces with one of the Veloki temples.

"I shall go," Augus announced.

I shook my head. "Riding there on horseback without rest would take a whole week. We don't know when the pope will make a move. It will be faster for me to go."

Beside me, Jane flinched.

Sorry, Jane. We have to sneak out one more time.

"Augus, please keep an eye on the situation at the imperial palace from here."

I figured that this would be no problem for someone who had been serving Rodrigo for so long.

"I shall do my best."

That was that. I stood from my seat. It was enough that

I had alerted the Erhart Manor staff of the danger ahead. If anything happened now, I was sure Augus would take care of the staff.

"Oh, the gifts!"

I turned to look at Augus, pausing even though I was already halfway out the door. He came to a halt behind me, about to escort me out.

"Yes? Go ahead, Lady Estella."

"I don't need them right now. He can give them to me himself when he comes back."

"But..."

Is he worried about going against an order from Rodrigo?

"Don't worry. I will tell him myself when I see him," I comforted Augus, who seemed uneasy, and headed back to Kartina Manor.

However, that night, as I crept carefully, slowly through the manor to sneak out once again... I was caught.

"Where are you going, Estella?"

By Kalen.

CHAPTER
THIRTY-SIX

"Where are you going, Estella?"

It was late. At this hour, the fourth and fifth floors of the Kartina Manor were usually quiet, which is why I tiptoed down the hallway as quietly as possible. Still, then a door suddenly opened, and Kalen called out to me. Completely startled, I froze on the spot and exchanged glances with Jane.

Should we run?

No, My Lady. If you run now, you may get locked in your room.

Haa... What do we do?

I turned around slowly, trying to put on a natural smile as I faced Kalen.

"Kalen, what are you doing up so late?"

"I couldn't sleep." He eyed us. "Estella, just like you said, it's late. Where are you going?"

"I was thirsty."

I blurted out a completely illogical excuse. It was worse than not saying anything.

Kalen frowned, demanding, "Jane, are you not doing your job in assisting your mistress? Why does Estella have to go get her own water?"

Predictably, Jane was caught in the crossfire. She bowed low and apologized before going downstairs, saying she would fetch me some water.

"I'll wait for you downstairs," she whispered to me before she left.

"You are too soft on the household staff, Estella. I know you treat Jane like a friend because you grew up together, but you know she's a servant, right?"

"Yes, Kalen, I know. I just couldn't sleep."

I hoped that Jane would manage to gather the things we had thrown out the window while I responded to Kalen.

"How about we take a walk together then?" Kalen's eyes lit up with the suggestion.

"No!" I said too quickly. "I... I suddenly feel sleepy. It must be because seeing you made me feel so at ease."

"Oh... All right then."

I wondered whether I should've just gone on a walk with him as I saw how disappointed he looked. Still, I couldn't delay my departure much longer.

"Let me escort you," Kalen insisted on accompanying me to my room, which was only three doors down.

I hurried, and we reached the door in a heartbeat.

"Sweet dreams, Kalen."

"Estella, wait."

Just as I opened the door to go inside, Kalen held me back.

Did he find out?

I asked carefully, "What is it?"

Kalen looked at me for a long moment before shaking his head.

"You really are beautiful. Let's meet in our dreams." He gave me a beguiled look before returning to his room.

They're all so obsessed with me.

I slammed the door and contemplated the situation. I didn't feel like risking going through the hallway again now that Kalen had caught me.

What should I do? I mulled it repeatedly in my head as I walked to and fro in my room. Then I remembered how Rodrigo had entered my room—through the window.

If he can do it, so can I.

I peered out through the window. I could see Jane some ways away, gathering our things. I couldn't just jump down. Instead, I took out the rope I kept under my bed. Carefully but as quickly as I could, I attached it to a pillar and then tied it securely around myself. Then, I skillfully rappelled out of the window.

I used the wall as support as I slowly worked my way down, one step at a time.

"My Lady!"

I had lowered myself without looking down and ended up on top of Jane. We collapsed into a pile.

"Sorry, Jane," I apologized.

"Let's hurry."

I led the way.

Although it hadn't been their fault, the portal maintenance staff must have been scolded after my last escape—the portal security was much more fortified this time. I used the tranquilizer darts I had prepared to put the guards to sleep. Once they were out, Jane swiftly retrieved the darts from them.

Jane and I made a perfect team. We could go down to the basement, where the portals were kept, in no time.

"M-m-my Lady!"

The person in charge of the portals had been nodding off when he caught sight of me. His skin flushed as pale as if he had just seen the grim reaper. He eyed me warily as he snatched at the bell pull, but Jane knocked him out cold with a quick whack to the back of the head.

Wow, look at her.

I searched the portal manager's pockets and fished out the key.

Poor guy. He'll get punished again for this.

I justified it by concluding that sacrifice was needed for a great cause. I glanced at him once more and then opened the door to the portals.

"They'll know where we went anyway, so let's not waste mana and just go there straight away."

"Good idea."

I stared at the map for a while before inputting the location on the portal. Straight to Rodrigo's tent.

"Ahhh!"

The portal that opened in the sky practically spat me out. I floundered in the air, looking completely ridiculous. This was all because I had put in a location on a map instead of selecting a specific portal to arrive at.

Am I going to die? I hope there are a bunch of trees beneath me to break my fall. I don't want to die here.

Covering my face with my arms, I did my best to protect my head as I fell.

Splash.

Fortunately, I landed in the lake.

Although the impact was still overwhelming, it was much better than landing on hard ground. Just as I felt relieved, I remembered that I had never learned how to swim.

Damn it.

I flailed, helpless. The water kept entering my nose and mouth. My dress floated to the surface and covered my face. The waterlogged fabric was heavy and began to weigh me down. I tried to paddle with my legs to keep afloat, but my feet were caught between the skirts of my dress, making it hard to move.

I guess this is how I die.

The water was in my eyes, nose, in my mouth and throat. I couldn't breathe! I began to lose consciousness, and my body went limp.

Then, someone grabbed my arm and yanked me to the surface. Air burst into my lungs.

"Estella! Estella!"

Someone desperately called to me. I managed to open my eyes to see who it was.

"Oh, Rodrigo."

With that, I lost consciousness.

"Rodrigo!"

I wrenched open my eyes.

I fell into the lake. I remember seeing Rodrigo's face. I sat up on the bed, dressed neatly in sleepwear. *How is this possible?*

Returning to my senses, I assessed my surroundings. A large map, a chair covered in an animal's fur, a large creaky bed, and a familiar robe. It was Rodrigo's tent.

"Are you awake?"

Rodrigo entered, holding a bowl of warm soup. The scent of the vegetables wafted toward me.

"They said it would be best for you to eat once you woke up."

He sat next to me and pushed the whole tray with the bowl of soup in my direction.

"I'll get up."

When I tried to get up, Rodrigo shook his head.

"You had a fever all night."

"I did?" *But I feel fine.*

"It must have been a great shock to your body to fall out of the sky and into water. And you nearly drowned."

All he was doing was stating the facts in a low voice, but I felt myself getting smaller and smaller with guilt.

"I really am fine."

"You are only feeling fine because of this."

Rodrigo lifted his hand. A blue light emanated from his palm.

Magic.

"I used healing magic," he said. "Does that bother you?"

"Not at all!"

"I will start to space out the intervals between using magic, so you should eat before then and get better."

Rodrigo took a spoonful of soup and raised it to my lips. I looked down at the spoon.   "Say 'ah.'"

I eyed him skeptically but opened my mouth. Considering this was a battlefield, the food was quite tasty.

"I recruited a chef," Rodrigo said as I swallowed and reached for another bite.

He pushed my hand away, and I let him lift the spoon again.

"From where?" I asked between spoonfuls.

"That is a secret."

He had many secrets. Rodrigo continued to feed me patiently, gently. I wasn't *that* sick...was I? Still, the soup bowl was soon empty.

"What brings you here? Again," he prompted.

"I take it that you're not happy to see me?"

He shut his mouth. I had been trying to lighten the mood, but it went cold instead. I picked up the wet cloth next to me and dabbed my mouth. I hesitated a moment, clearing my throat.

"Emperor Thereo is on the move."

"Because the Veloki Kingdom is crowning a new king?"

"Oh, so you knew?"

"I was the one behind it."

Rodrigo began to explain the details of what he had been doing to end this war. Listening intently, I responded with exclamations and whines of disappointment.

Finally, I announced, "It's a good plan."

"Your future husband is more competent than you think. Though you might have thought him incompetent as of late."

"I've always thought you competent," I said honestly.

Rodrigo turned away. Maybe it was because I was sick, but the tips of his ears looked red.

"That's not why I came," I explained. "I came to let you know that you are in danger of being labeled a heretic. The pope is going to arrive soon."

"Labeled a heretic?" Rodrigo asked.

"Can you think of anything that might have started that rumor?"

Rodrigo quieted, thinking. He tended to tap his fingers against something when he was deep in thought. This time, it was the bedside table. I found myself focusing on the rhythmical tapping.

"Gunther." Rodrigo's fingers stopped as he looked at me, apparently remembering something. "We visited a temple because he needed healing."

"Gunther got hurt?"

Jane would be so upset to hear that. Worry sparked in my chest.

I asked, "Come to think of it, where is Jane? Did you see her?"

"The person who came with you ended up crashing into a tree canopy instead of the lake. Fortunately, the foliage broke her fall. I gave her a small tent to stay in."

Thank goodness. Jane is okay overall.

I told Rodrigo, "Please let her know that I asked about her as soon as I woke up, in case she asks."

He let out a chuckle, nodding.

Phew.

"But anyway, please tell me more about what happened with Gunther."

Rodrigo's explained that Gunther had been hurt, and the camp had been too far to reach because he had been bleeding too much. He needed more than simple medical attention, so they ended up going to the temple. The priests at the temple helped, even though they knew they were from the empire. With their help, Gunther recovered to head back to the war camp.

"Thank goodness. How did he get hurt?"

Rodrigo took out a small box from the bedside table drawer. He opened the lid. Inside was a small ball of thin, transparent thread.

"Oh, this is…"

"Do you know what it is?"

"Can I take a look?"

"It's dangerous."

"I'll be fine."

I took hold of the thread and looked at it closely. It originated from a type of monster called the spiness. Spiness thread was transparent but as strong as steel. Because it was hard to detect due to its transparency, it was often used in traps made by assassins. Most of the time, they set it up at ankle height to handicap but not kill the target. When set up at neck height, the thread could be used to slay dozens at a time.

It was fortunate, therefore, that it was hard to come by and extremely expensive, seeing how dangerous it was.

"This was set up in the forests of the Veloki Kingdom?"

Rodrigo nodded. Spiness thread was an item monopolized by the empire. I knew this because the Kartinas oversaw the production and sale of this particular product.

Perhaps the Kartinas had smuggled some of it out.

No. Byproducts of monsters were strictly regulated. The related ledgers were carefully and meticulously kept before being checked by the emperor. There was only one suspect. Emperor Thereo had handed this over to someone in the Veloki Kingdom.

"You know something," Rodrigo said, watching my expression change.

"I think I may have just found a perfect bargaining chip."

I told Rodrigo everything I knew about spiness thread. His smile grew wider and wider.

"He started this war but provided supplies to the other side so that they would win. This could be a fatal blow. However..."

"However?"

CHAPTER
THIRTY-SEVEN

"That's not enough to sway Emperor Thereo."

Of course not.

"If things go wrong, they might blame your family."

Hm? That's not good. Tension grew between my eyebrows, my worry evolving into a headache. This was serious.

"It's probably best to hide this evidence."

Rodrigo extracted the thread from my hands and delicately replaced it in the box. Then he went to put it back inside the bedside table drawer. I grabbed him by the wrist.

"No, let's try to use it."

He tilted his head to one side.

"I'm going to save both my family and you. So please, give me that."

My plan was reckless, but I remembered what Emperor Thereo was like in the novel. Emotional and selfish, but demanding respect. It was very emperor-like of him. All I had to do was satisfy that selfishness a little.

I wasn't sure whether I could manage this, but I had to try. I wouldn't let anyone die. Not my family. Not Rodrigo.

"Estella!"

At ease with a full belly and Rodrigo at my side, I must have fallen asleep. I woke to someone shaking my shoulder.

Outside, a commotion caught my attention, but Jane demanded it first.

"My Lady, they're all here!"

Her eyes were wide, and she removed her hand from my shoulder to raise it to her face nervously.

I knew who she meant.

"All right. I'm coming," I said.

"There's no need for you to get up, Estella."

Rodrigo grabbed me as I tried to get up and made me lie down again. He even pulled the blanket over me. As he tenderly patted the blanket to tuck me in, I stared beyond him at the entrance.

The tent opened with a flutter, and waves of heat rolled in. Kalen, Ada, and Ayla barged inside, all looking furious. Huffing in agitation, Ada yanked out a dagger and chucked it across the tent without warning. She was aiming for Rodrigo's neck.

Rodrigo's expression remained unchanged as he turned slightly. The knife whizzed by him. If he hadn't dodged just in time, blood would've started spraying everywhere.

"You bastard! How dare you dodge that! You should be begging for forgiveness!"

Ada's fists trembled.

"What use would it be to be forgiven after being killed?"

I covered my face with my hands. He was not wrong, but he didn't need to say it so annoyingly.

"Stand aside! How can you miss that?"

Next up was Ayla. She spat into her palms before leaning back and then sprinting forward. Once Rodrigo was within reach, Ayla raised her leg high and went for a drop kick—but Rodrigo easily evaded her attack as well. Instead, Ayla went flying and landed on the ground in front of Jane.

"I'm sorry, My Lady." Jane collapsed to her knees.

"I'll talk to you later!" Ayla snapped and sprang to her feet.

She brushed the dust from her clothes and leaped at Rodrigo again. I stopped her. She couldn't ignore my hand tugging on her clothes.

"Estella!"

She trembled with fury as she glared at Rodrigo but didn't try to attack him again.

Kalen was ready anyway. He roared in fury as he ran at Rodrigo and swung his fist. With a resounding *pow,* Rodrigo's face was pushed to the side. Kalen looked startled, as if he hadn't expected his punch to land.

"Rodrigo!"

I was startled too. He should have been able to dodge that punch, and I couldn't help thinking he must've taken the punch on purpose.

"Don't get up, Estella."

He wiped his bleeding lip with the back of his hand before looking at me with a smile.

"What's wrong with you? You could have easily dodged that!"

"Then you would've attacked me again, no?"

"So you're saying you took the punch on purpose?"

"I do feel like I deserved it a little."

Rodrigo languidly stretched his neck from side to side.

"If my sister were this lovely and had run away from home twice because of some guy, I would want to twist his head off as well."

His sweet words sounded chilling. It must have been the right thing to say because my siblings seemed to calm down slightly. They even nodded enthusiastically.

"But I won't take another hit. That really hurt." Rodrigo furrowed his eyebrows.

Wow, he's handsome even when he's frowning. My cheeks warmed. *Hey, why is he using his charm right now?*

"All I have is wine, but would you like a glass?"

Leaving my siblings standing there, exasperated and rooted to the spot, Rodrigo opened a small box. Heating a small ceramic pot and taking the time to brew tea was a completely unnecessary extravagance in a war camp. Rather, it was downright idiotic.

It was much more economical and reasonable to store bottles of alcohol where you would usually keep a tea set. Jane took the bottle Rodrigo had procured and placed it on the table. Kalen, Ada, and Ayla glared at Jane, who hiccupped nervously before shuffling over to my side.

"Estella, do you really like that bastard?"

All eyes were on me now. I sat up in bed and brushed back my disheveled hair. The answer was obvious.

"I do."

Rodrigo's eyebrows shot up for a moment before descending. My siblings' shoulders sagged exaggeratedly. A moment of silence followed.

"Enough to follow him to this pathetic war camp?"

Rodrigo seemed offended by his war camp's description and took half a step forward, but I shook my head. I also didn't think his war camp deserved to be called wretched, but I didn't want to antagonize Kalen further.

"I would go to even worse places just to see him."

However, he seemed more hurt by what I had to say. I

apologized to him inwardly, turning toward Rodrigo with a steady, loving gaze.

"Ha! Are you saying you'll stay here until the war is over?"

"I'm saying I'll be visiting frequently until the war is over."

I told a bit of a lie, feeling that Kalen might explode if I told him I would stay here for a while.

"Did you hear that, Ada?" Ayla mumbled in disbelief.

"Our beautiful sister wants to frequent this dirty and disgusting place!"

"No way! This place smells of dust and blood! She shouldn't be in such a place!"

I figured that Rodrigo must be annoyed to hear this from the people who went around making places smell exactly like that. Feeling slightly guilty, I shot him a glance.

"If I had known Estella was coming, I would have tidied up the place. Estella, would you let me know in advance the next time you visit again? I'll clean up the room and wash the blankets."

"Hey! There's absolutely no reason for you to wash the blankets!"

"She needs a place to rest when she is tired, don't you think?" As Rodrigo said this, he placed a hand on my shoulder.

Ayla and Ada went red in the face.

Whoa, wait. Stop imagining things, sisters!

"Why don't you all sit down? Must Estella keep looking up at you?"

He used me as an excuse to make my siblings sit at the table. Because it was often used for war meetings, Rodrigo's tent had plenty of chairs. Since there were more than enough chairs for all of us to sit in a circle, I nudged a chair toward Jane.

You have a seat too.

At my silent suggestion, Jane subtly shook her head and pointed toward the entrance.

Can I please leave? I'm suffocating in here, My Lady. I knew what she must be asking.

I waved my hand. *If you want to leave, now's your chance.*

Everyone was squabbling to sit next to me. Rodrigo rolled his eyes. It was embarrassing, but I let my siblings squabble for a moment. Jane took the opportunity to sneak out. Kalen, Ada, and Ayla all have poor memories. If I praised Jane before them, they would forget her fault soon enough.

I hoped for the best as I sat next to Rodrigo.

My siblings' frozen expressions were quite a sight to behold. Their resentful gazes focused on Rodrigo. He seemed slightly resentful at their apparent horror, but I gave everyone a small smile and flicked his thigh under the table.

Smile.

Rodrigo smiled brightly. I really couldn't figure out whether he was good at following my lead or not.

Our conversation, which mostly consisted of interrogating Rodrigo, dragged on. He had to repeat himself endlessly.

"*I like Estella a lot.*"

"*I will do anything for her.*"

"*I can't promise you I'll be able to stop her from coming here.*"

"So, what are you saying?!"

Ultimately, Kalen failed to hold back his anger and sprang to his feet.

"I am saying that there's nothing I can do."

"What do you mean, nothing? You have to stop Estella from coming here!"

I finally raised my hand, unable to keep listening to this infinitely repeating conversation. Everyone's eyes fixated on me.

I said, "Do you want me to tell you how to get me to stop coming here?"

"You'll stop coming?"

CHAPTER
THIRTY-EIGHT

Rodrigo asked, surprised and, apparently, a little sad.

Why do you sound disappointed? Uncomfortable situations like this happen whenever I come here. I shook my head. Kalen, Ada, and Ayla's eyes sparkled.

"You just have to end the war."

It was such a simple answer.

"Once Rodrigo returns to the capital, I won't come here anymore."

Kalen's jaw dropped. Ada followed suit. Then Ayla.

I looked at Rodrigo. *How's that? I did well, right?*

Rodrigo's expression was strange, as his lips curled into a smile, and he burst out laughing.

"You really are an amazing woman! I'm amused."

"Don't laugh. I'm being serious."

I figured it would be good if Kalen, Ada, and Ayla cooperated with Rodrigo to end this war faster. It would help the empire and make my family look good in the process.

"S-so, we just need to end this war, right?"

"I'll go see father."

"I'll go see the crown prince..."

Each of my siblings was ready to do their part. However, I had to stop Kalen.

"Not the crown prince."

"Why not?"

Emperor Thereo's military forces were strong. As the empire's leader, he controlled the largest army. He had many capable knights and even a few sorcerers. If the emperor decided to use his forces to aid in the war, it would be over in a heartbeat.

"If he wanted to step up, he would have done so already. I plan on having it out with the emperor himself by going to see him rather than the crown prince," I said, looking determined.

My siblings narrowed their eyes, trying to understand what I meant.

"I plan on blackmailing him instead of asking for help."

Their expressions hardened. Only Rodrigo was smiling as he looked at me. The affection in his gaze made me turn away from him, feeling warm again.

"Your Majesty, Lady Estella is here to request an audience. Sir Kalen is with her."

Emperor Thereo frowned as he woke to the attendant's call.

The morning light was too bright through the open curtains. It had been a while since he had been able to relax, but having heard the previous night that Rodrigo wasn't doing well in battle, he had had a drink and slept soundly.

"It's far too early," the emperor said sharply, at which the attendant bowed.

"She said it was urgent."

They were the children of a noble with no titles of their own. It was unlikely for him to see them even if they had sent a messenger ahead of time, so it was daring of them simply to barge into the palace like this.

Even considering that they were the children of a noble family he kept at his side, Emperor Thereo didn't see why he should allow for such deviance from formalities.

"Tell them to leave and wait for my correspondence."

It was a sign of respect for the Kartinas that Thereo didn't punish them severely for their insolence.

"Your Majesty, Lady Estella asked me to deliver this to you if you refused to meet with her."

The attendant's hand, quivering, extended with a box. It was already a great transgression for him to relay Estella's message instead of carrying out the emperor's orders immediately, but the attendant recalled Kalen's menacing glare.

"I'm going to kill you if you do not deliver it properly."

In his twenty years of service at the imperial palace, the attendant had met many a character. Still, it had been a while since he had seen eyes like Kalen's.

He's a mad dog.

Emperor Thereo was a dog as well, but at least he wasn't mad, so the attendant had chosen to delay the emperor's orders. And that decision had been the right one to make.

"Th-this is... Let her in this instant!"

Emperor Thereo opened the box and gasped.

I sipped the tea Emperor Thereo's attendant had served. The tea had cooled just enough to be pleasantly warm. Kalen sipped his too. A breeze came in through the windows of the emperor's room and made the golden curtains flutter. It was a peaceful scene, but I was suddenly reminded of Rodrigo, who must be suffering out on the battlefield. My eyebrows furrowed at the thought.

"What is going on?" Emperor Thereo's voice was low and dignified, but it had a slight tremble.

He's agitated.

I glanced at the box the emperor was touching with the tips of his fingers.

"Does my gift suit your taste, Your Majesty?"

"Does your father, Count Kartina, know about this?"

We were talking past each other. The emperor's mouth was turned up in a smile, but his eyes were seething.

"My father is busy exterminating monsters at your command." *I came here without telling him. So what?*

"I am certainly aware of how much your family sacrifices for the empire. Your family always works hard."

Emperor Thereo spoke as if he was congratulating me as he raised his teacup. What he meant was clear.

You are my vassals, so stop misbehaving and obey me.

"Your Majesty," I said. "I do not disagree with you. That is precisely why I have come to the imperial palace so early in the morning with this box in tow."

I bowed my head. Showing the top of your head to someone indicated surrender. Emperor Thereo didn't see me as worthy of respect anyway. I was just a young girl without a title of her own and not even a husband.

It wasn't exactly the world I used to live in, not really. Here, a woman's status was completely dependent on her parents and her husband. For nobles, it wasn't as harsh, but being respected was another matter entirely.

And by Emperor Thereo at that.

I wasn't here to stand tall in front of Emperor Thereo, so this didn't bother me, but it did seem to bother Kalen.

"Your Majesty, when Count Kartina is absent, he entrusts his duties to his children. Especially when he is away exterminating monsters."

In other words, both Kalen and I held the position of count. His words reminded the emperor not to disregard us. I found myself in awe of Kalen for having the guts to stand up to the old lion of an emperor who ruled the empire leisurely on his back.

"The future of the Kartinas looks bright." He laughed. "All right. Go ahead and tell me what it is that you want from me."

I grit my teeth at how the emperor straightened up so he could look down as he addressed my brother. Still, I didn't want my petty emotions to ruin anything.

"Someone is going behind your back and making deals during this war."

Emperor Thereo's brow twitched.

"The box you are holding contains a weapon that the Kartinas produced solely to protect Your Majesty and the empire. I'm sure you are familiar with it."

He couldn't possibly feign ignorance. The imperial family had sent money to the Kartinas to develop this weapon.

"Yes. Continue."

"The Kartinas offer this product only to the imperial family, Your Majesty. However, this was found on one of the ruffians of the Veloki Kingdom."

"Do you have proof?"

"Sir Rodrigo's right-hand man was injured."

I had expected Emperor Thereo to say he didn't believe the evidence, but he stayed quiet.

"Go on."

"I have a question for you. How did a product of our family end up in Veloki's hands?"

"Are you asking for an internal investigation of the Kartinas?"

He was pushing back. However, I didn't even blink.

"An internal investigation of the imperial palace may be necessary as well."

"Are you suggesting that someone would dare to pocket an item right under my nose?"

"That must be what happened unless it was your direct order, Your Majesty."

Emperor Thereo glowered at me for a long moment in silence, leaning back against the couch. His red eyes glinted dangerously, and his posture was stiff.

"Will you take responsibility for these claims?"

"I will take all the responsibility I owe, and if there is anything I must be held responsible for, I shall do so."

"What about you?"

The question was directed at Kalen. He nodded as he answered, "The Kartinas will show a united front, Your Majesty."

Emperor Thereo picked up the box, studying it, likely considering all that had been said. I raised my teacup and finished the cold tea in one gulp. Though I had been nervous when I first faced the emperor, my anxiety had now died down, and my muscles weren't so tense.

Maybe that tension had been transferred to Emperor Thereo. He hadn't moved for a while but began fidgeting more and more, as if uncomfortable in his seat.

"I will have it looked into," he finally said.

The results of that investigation were obvious. They would conclude that someone from the imperial palace had stolen the item. The emperor would never blame himself.

"Please allow the Kartinas to head this investigation, Your Majesty."

I knew what Emperor Thereo thought as his brows lifted up in surprise and then furrowed deeply. Time for my next move.

"The Kartinas?" Emperor Thereo grimaced outright, clearly displeased by the idea.

"It is a product made by the Kartinas. Though we offered it up to you, if this item is used with ill intent, our family will be blamed."

"Since when are the Kartinas so concerned with the opinions of others? You are my—"

"Isn't it necessary to be cautious exactly because we are Your Majesty's right hand?" I interrupted the emperor.

It was a crime to interrupt him, but Thereo did not point this out. Even he knew just how fond the Kartinas were of me. *He also knows that he can't make enemies of the Kartinas yet.* Emperor Thereo was greedy, not stupid. Rather, his intelligence was the issue.

"What is it that you want?" Emperor Thereo said, his glare deadly.

Finally, the words I had been waiting for.

"I request fair treatment for Sir Rodrigo."

"He is at war. If he succeeds, he will be rewarded accordingly, and if he loses, he will be held responsible."

"I trust that you will treat him fairly."

I would ensure that he won the war anyway. No matter what.

I stood up from my seat. Emperor Thereo stopped me as I tried to reach for the box. The emperor and I looked at each other, both of us resting a hand on the box. His red eyes narrowed as his face crinkled into a smile. Emperor Thereo had regained his composure.

"I trust the Kartinas," he said.

"As is your right."

Emperor Thereo removed his hand and leaned back at my answer.

"Leave the box."

So he wants to cover this up.

As I looked at him curiously, my head tilted to the side, Emperor Thereo laughed.

"What a smart girl. You are too good for Rodrigo."

"I will take that as a compliment."

I hurriedly curtsied, worried that Emperor Thereo would try to match me up with the crown prince. He didn't stop us from leaving.

In the carriage on our way home, Kalen didn't say much. The creases on his forehead when he frowned made him seem conflicted.

"When did you grow up so much, my dear sister?"

I exhaled a chuckle at his mumbled words. Kalen was not concerned about why I was standing up against Emperor Thereo or what would happen to the Kartinas from now on. All he was worried about was that I was maturing too fast and would no longer need him. That was it.

"I still have a lot to learn."

Kalen lowered his elbow from where it had been leaning against the windowsill and turned to look at me. It was fascinating to see myself reflected in his eyes, which looked just like mine.

"I will help you with anything. Don't worry."

Though he had no idea I was deceiving him, his words were comforting. I hadn't realized I needed reassurance, but this felt like a small gift.

"Thank you, Kalen. You helped a lot today too."

Even though Kalen had his own reasons for wanting to end this war quickly—so he could stop me from meeting Rodrigo—ultimately, he had gone with me to blackmail Emperor Thereo in the Kartinas' name. Had I been part of any other family, I would have been confined to my room just for suggesting such a thing.

Instead, he had not only supported me but even joined me. It wouldn't have been possible without his love for and trust in me.

Still gazing intently, Kalen's eyes teared up. He dabbed at his eyes with his fingertips as he mumbled, "Something must've gotten in my eyes."

I turned my head away to allow Kalen some privacy in case he was embarrassed about shedding tears from being so moved. It was time to see Rodrigo.

The sun had only just risen, and the clouds were tinged in pink. In the dim early morning light, Rodrigo patrolled the area with a troop of seasoned soldiers. The enemy troops hadn't moved for a few days. It was too quiet, as if they were ready to give up after being attacked daily.

Rodrigo knew very well that this was all the more reason to keep his guard up. He predicted the enemy was taking the time to reorganize forces before a large-scale attack.

And Rodrigo was right. Back from the patrol, he pulled off his helmet just as he heard a cry.

"General, o-over there!"

The sound of hooves rang out like thunder. Dust rose in thick clouds. There had been no signs of movement during their patrol, but Rodrigo's suspicions were proving true. He ripped the long telescope from the soldier's hands and raised it to his eye. As he lowered the telescope, his expression darkened.

"Those lunatics."

CHAPTER
THIRTY-NINE

He cursed reflexively. Through the telescope, he spied a crowd of ragged slaves. Children were among them, and they were all running toward Rodrigo and his men, completely unarmed. They had caught sight of what appeared to be a group of beggars on their patrol.

"I thought they were refugees, escaping from the war..." Rodrigo muttered.

It was a dirty, pathetic tactic to send out slaves in battle, not only untrained but unarmed. It could hardly be called a tactic. Rodrigo shook his head.

"Do we have to attack them?" Devlon asked, his face twisting into a grimace.

The other commanders were also waiting for Rodrigo's answer.

"They are being used as shields. Pay attention to the soldiers behind them," Rodrigo said, handing the telescope to the commander beside him.

Just as he had said, toward the rear of the band of slaves were knights on horseback, carrying spears. The answer was clear. If they didn't kill the slaves, they would die. There was no alternative.

Rodrigo squeezed his eyes shut and snapped, "Minimize our losses and move back."

"Are you telling us to retreat?" asked a commander sporting a long, white beard.

He was someone who had achieved quite a few victories during this war. Indeed, he was such a competent commander that it was hard to believe Emperor Thereo had sent him.

"If we retreat now, we lose. We have been defending this territory tooth and nail!"

Rodrigo looked at him and raised the corners of his lips.

"There are many ways to win a war. I am simply choosing the most efficient way." Rodrigo adjusted his grip on his sword.

Devlon's gaze wavered. He stood in Rodrigo's way as if he could tell what he was planning to do.

"You must not."

"You can only earn great victories by overcoming great dangers." Rodrigo pushed Devlon aside.

At the same time, he handed him the badge that indicated full authority over the army to Devlon.

"I will be back after I behead the enemy general." Rodrigo leaped onto his horse.

By the time the others understood what he had meant,

Rodrigo had already ridden ahead—toward the enemy.

"Everyone, keep an eye on the situation as you move back. If your life is in danger, defend yourself whether or not the enemy is armed, but do not kill indiscriminately. Is that clear?" Devlon exclaimed.

Because of the badge Rodrigo handed him, Devlon couldn't go after him. It had become his duty to lead before all else.

"General Versillo, please protect His Grace," he asked the white-bearded general.

He was going to die. However, he wouldn't die in vain. Devlon trusted that the general would save Rodrigo's life at least once.

The white-bearded General Versillo let out a huff of laughter.

"You look like you're about to die. How are you going to survive until I get back?"

Despite this, General Versillo hopped on his horse and raced after Rodrigo. A few knights followed suit.

Devlon clenched his fists. *If Gunther were here...* He shook his head and dismissed the thought. All they could do now was trust Rodrigo.

Stefan had come home. These days, he had to leave more frequently to take care of the monsters in the western region.

It had been a while since the whole family was home at the same time. Hela glanced Stefan up and down before hugging him. Ada, Ayla, and Kalen bowed their heads.

Since Stefan had to go to the western border more often, I was able to visit Rodrigo, but it wasn't all good. *What's happening at the western border?*

"I will be gone for a while to exterminate the monsters in the western region. Hela will come with me."

Something was definitely up. We were curious, but we kept our mouths shut. Instead, we exchanged glances as we kept our heads bowed.

"I heard you visited the emperor while I was gone, Kalen," Stefan observed.

That blabbermouth. I inwardly cursed the emperor and pretended to take a sip of water as I eyed Stefan.

"Yes," Kalen replied simply. "His Majesty had done something to endanger the Kartinas, so I went to see him."

"The Kartinas? Or the Erharts?" Stefan's eyes narrowed.

The dining room went quiet. I put down my cup.

"The empire, Father." My tone was resolute.

Stefan's gaze rested on me. The annoyance in his eyes seemed to melt away. "If you say so, my darling. But Estella, I'm worried."

I tipped my head.

"I am worried that you may risk the emperor's wrath while your mother and I are gone."

What on earth did that bastard of an emperor tell Stefan to make him worry so much? That old fox... I really despised him. What came next was a long scolding from Stefan. At the end of it, he told us that the monsters at the western border were acting unusually. *Monsters in the west, monsters in the west...* I didn't realize I was mumbling to myself as I contemplated this.

"Estella?" Ayla eyed me closely.

I squished my face into a smile.

"You can't go to the western border, okay? You're too curious," she said.

Why didn't I think of going there? I nodded just to comfort Ayla.

Hela and Stefan headed to the western border at dawn the next morning. I rose to watch them go, observing a fair number of troops leaving with them.

"Why are they taking the road instead of a portal?"

"I heard the sorcerers have lost a lot of mana," Jane told me, probably having heard the rumor from the other household staff.

"Mana?"

Insufficient mana was a bad sign. In the novel, it meant

that Rodrigo was about to go berserk. *Which meant...*

"Something must've happened to Rodrigo!"

Jane gave me a strange look as I sprang to my feet.

"His grace is on the battlefield, where things are bound to happen to him."

I shook my head at Jane, who looked at me as if I was overreacting.

"He must be in danger."

"So you're going to go save him like a knight in shining armor?"

"Yes, of course."

"Please, my lady. I don't want to be punished again."

Jane had been punished for copying the Kartina history book by hand three times because she had accompanied me last time. To Jane, who much preferred her usual chores over repetitive bookwork, this had been a huge punishment. Her hands still smelled of ink.

"You don't need to come with me."

Jane sighed deeply. "I'll get killed if I don't."

"That's settled, then."

I stepped out of my nightgown.

Jane sighed again but rummaged through the wardrobe to pick out a comfortable dress for me. I retrieved a pair of pants from under the bed.

"My Lady?"

"I'm going to wear pants underneath. I have a bad feeling."

The sorcerers losing their mana. The monsters acting strangely at the western border. That border was shared with the Veloki kingdom.

"If you're going to go, hurry up. Morning training will start soon."

Jane retrieved my luggage from the closet. She hefted it toward me.

"You packed already?" I asked, observing its weight.

"I never unpacked."

"You're so smart, Jane."

Jane exhaled a sigh that could've put out a fire. "It's all thanks to you."

It didn't really sound like a compliment, but I didn't chide Jane and instead stepped out of my room.

Rodrigo leaned against a tree's trunk and took deep breaths. A whole day had passed since he had charged at the enemy commander, swearing to behead him. The sun had set, and a new day, with new opportunities and new knowledge, had dawned.

A sorcerer.

Rodrigo brushed his dirty hand through his hair. He had made it close to the enemy commander. It hadn't been difficult to get past the slaves because they were charging straight ahead, completely disregarding him, as if they had been drugged.

When he had reached the enemy knights, he was able to get through easily, thanks to General Versillo and the knights who had followed him. It hadn't taken long to get to the middle of the enemy army. The issue had been the enemy general himself.

"A powerful sorcerer," Rodrigo muttered.

The general towered over every soldier with his enormous frame. His skin was too pale, and his teeth were sharp like a lion's when he grinned at Rodrigo. He had heard of sorcerers who could use magic to strengthen and even modify their bodies. Still, such magic was, of course, forbidden across the continent.

Entranced, briefly, by the strange sight of the general, Rodrigo snapped back to his senses and charged. The general used magic.

Rodrigo went flying and crashed against a tree trunk. His head smashed against the wood, knocking him unconscious. And that was where he had woken up, sitting beneath that tree. Fortunately, nothing was broken since he had used a magic shield instinctively.

Rodrigo stood carefully at first, as his muscles adjusted to the bruising. Using a sorcerer, and one who used dark magic at that, was a clear offense.

I have to talk to Franz.

Rodrigo closed his eyes and flexed his hand. His horse was gone. The only way to return quickly to the war camp now was magic.

When I arrived at Rodrigo's tent, it was empty. There weren't any soldiers, either. The war camp had been trampled to shreds. Where was everyone? I looked out across the scattered debris, at a loss for words.

"Did they lose?"

I shook my head at Jane's question. "If they had lost, we would have heard about it."

They would have raised a flag.

"But this..."

"They retreated."

There were too few bodies around for them to have fought over the war camp. Besides, the bodies there were not any of Rodrigo's men. My eyes glossed over with tears with grief for the dead and relief at who, I hoped, was still alive.

As I studied them, I observed, "How strange."

"What?"

"All these people look like serfs."

"Stop staring at those corpses, My Lady. It's terrifying."

Jane sometimes talked like she wasn't part of the Kartina household.

I glanced over at her and straightened up. Then I looked around. There were more than a few strange things about this place.

If they had retreated because they had been pushed back, the Velokian army would have overtaken the war camp, but no one was there. It was too tidy for there to have been fighting going on but too messy for them to have simply moved their camp.

"My head hurts." I crossed my arms and looked around.

"Huh? My Lady!" Jane suddenly exclaimed, pointing above.

I looked up just in time to see Rodrigo fall out of the air and plummet toward us. He thumped heavily onto the ground nearby.

"Rodrigo!"

CHAPTER
FORTY

He was a complete mess, but he managed to clamber to his feet after the fall. Dazed, he peered at Jane and me. First, his eyes widened in surprise, and then his brows knit tightly in concern. He stalked toward me.

"What are you doing here?"

I could tell just how much he had gone through by the crack in his voice.

I said, "I could ask you the same thing. What happened here?"

I gestured around us, and Rodrigo put his dirty hand on his forehead.

"It's a long story," he said.

We found a few chairs intact and set them up for us to rest beneath Rodrigo's collapsed tent. He briefly explained what had happened, but his explanation lacked detail since he wasn't quite sure what had happened, either.

I asked for more information a few times, but he simply shrugged.

"I see."

Once he was done explaining, I noticed how pale his face was. *Come to think of it, he said he took a huge hit from a sorcerer.*

"Jane, water."

Jane rummaged through our bags and retrieved a bottle of water, opening it to wet a handkerchief. Rodrigo was staring out across the empty camp.

"Look at me." I stood in front of him and raised his chin with my fingers.

Rodrigo looked up. His red eyes met mine.

"They say the world's greatest sorcerer has red eyes," I said.

Rodrigo released a chuckle.

I guess he thinks I'm trying to comfort him. I had only expressed a fact. He was despairing over his first defeat. More than anything, the guilt of failing to protect those who had trusted him enough to follow him into battle must have been weighing on him. I raised the handkerchief and wiped away the sweat and dust on his face.

"Did I look so unseemly?"

"Didn't I tell you? You would look handsome even with filth all over your face."

Rodrigo chuckled slightly at my joke. I knew my words wouldn't reach him right now, no matter what I said. My heart ached. Once I had wiped away most of the dirt, he took my hand and lowered it from his face.

"Go back." He was serious.

"I'm stronger than you think," I said.

"You are unbelievably competent, yes."

"If you're aware of that, shouldn't you be begging me to stay?"

I twisted my wrist out of his grip and began to wipe his cheek with the other side of the handkerchief. His face was weirdly clean for someone who had spent months on the battlefield. Just a few wipes would have been enough, but I somehow felt compelled to touch his face. It would be weird to do so without an excuse, so I needed the handkerchief.

Jane shot a glance at me before shuffling away. She put some distance between us, enough so that she could still see us but just out of earshot.

Rodrigo leaned down toward me after he saw that Jane had gone far enough away.

Much closer now, he hurriedly whispered, "I do not want you to stay at a dangerous place like this. Did I not tell you I would propose to you on your birthday?"

Now that I thought about it, my birthday was coming up soon. Back when he had made the promise, it had sounded like Rodrigo would return quickly, but the war had gone on and on and turned into a war of attrition.

"Then I'll be the first woman to be proposed to on the

battlefield," I said, dismissing his worries—but he grabbed my hand again tightly.

"Estella." His red-eyed gaze wavered.

I gazed into his eyes; they seemed to tremble with self-hatred.

He said, "I told you I would be back by then."

"So you want me to sit back while you suffer like this?"

He nodded.

"Do you want me to be some silly noblewoman playing house while you risk your life out here?" I raised my voice inadvertently.

I clenched my fists, leaning away from him. Why couldn't he just rely on me sometimes?

"That's not what I—"

"If that's the kind of woman you wanted, you've chosen wrong," I snapped. "I'm not that kind of person."

I snatched my hand from Rodrigo's grip and called for Jane, who had tactfully walked away from us while I had cleaned his face. She saw me angrily brush my hand through my hair and helped me tie it up.

"Jane, give me the magic paper."

"Pardon? But it'll reveal your location, My Lady."

The Kartinas used magic paper when there was a need to communicate quickly. When you wrote on it and burned it, the writing would appear on a designated piece of paper somewhere else. However, the sender's location would also appear. It made sense because the recipient needed to know where the sender was to reply.

"My siblings already know where I am anyway."

This was already the third time. They'd have to be stupid not to know where I was. They might have given up on stopping me, seeing as they hadn't chased me down already.

Jane made no more comments as she took the magic paper and magic ink from my bag. I looked around. There was nothing that could be used as a writing desk.

My eyes met Rodrigo's. I huffed, stepped closer to him, and lightly pushed his shoulder. He leaned over slowly. I held the paper against his bent back.

"My Lady! What are you doing?!"

Rodrigo wasn't complaining, but Jane seemed upset. I used his broad back as a flat surface to write a message.

The main office of the Mave Guild, owned by the Kartinas, was always noisy and bustling. Just validating the massive amount of information flowing in from all over the empire and sorting it by the degree of importance was a major task. Since the guild also ran errands, those had to be taken care of as well.

Porter oversaw the guild's busiest sector. He was also someone who answered to Estella. He watched patiently as a message from Estella began to write itself on the magic paper on his desk.

"There's suspicious movement in the Veloki Kingdom. Find me evidence, however small, of any changes."

Porter scratched his head, frowning. *What is she doing, and where is she that she needs information on a place the Kartinas have labeled top priority?* Her locations blipped on the small map for a moment.

"On the battlefield? She must've finally gone insane!" Porter sprang to his feet.

Sweeping all the documents containing information on the Veloki Peninsula into a bag, he hurried out the door to head to the Kartina Manor.

Estella had called for him, so he had no choice. He hated the idea of meeting Stefan and Hela, but he would have to use their portal under Estella's name. *Otherwise...* Porter shuddered.

He grumbled, walking faster, "I hate horses."

We decided to stay in Rodrigo's tent. Jane said it was too dangerous, but Rodrigo and I simultaneously shook our heads.

"They won't come back."

I agreed with Rodrigo. He added that if someone were to return, it would be Devlon. Still, Jane fidgeted.

She must be curious about Gunther. I casually asked Rodrigo how Gunther was doing.

"Oh, he's... fine."

Rodrigo's slight pause was suspicious, but the fact that he was alive was more than enough. I patted Jane's hand to comfort her.

Rodrigo wandered around the camp as we gathered anything useful. With just a few movements, an awning was put up to better hold the ruined tent above our heads, and soft cushions were procured for our chairs. He managed to cobble together a table to put things on and was now boiling water in a kettle he had found.

"It's like magic."

I knew he hadn't used any magic as he worked. However, it certainly felt magical when he managed to procure all of this so quickly.

"Didn't you know? Your lover is a sorcerer."

"I did, but I didn't know he'd be so useful."

Steam soon began to rise from the kettle. Rodrigo poured hot water into a few cups he had washed. *I know Porter will come here since I called for him. I just don't know how long—*

A loud noise interrupted my train of thought. It wasn't far from where Rodrigo had put up an awning for us. As we emerged from it, we caught sight of Porter, who had fallen on his face, and Ada, who was picking him up by the back of his shirt. Ayla was with them too.

"Your brother isn't here today," Rodrigo said, sounding not at all surprised.

"Our parents are busy, you see."

I figured that Kalen wouldn't be able to leave the manor since our parents had put him in charge before they left for the western border.

"Ada! Ayla!" I ran to my sisters and gave them a big hug to calm them down.

They hugged me back tightly and took a few deep breaths.

"You must've had such a hard time, Estella! Coming to a terrible place like... Wait, what happened here? It's even worse than last time. I don't even know what to say."

I smiled wordlessly at her harsh assessment of the camp.

"Did you lose?" Ayla asked, looking at Rodrigo.

He looked up and stared at her. "Not yet."

"That sounds like it's just a matter of time."

I tried to catch Ayla's attention with a look, but Ada was

standing between us and blocking my view of her.

"Aren't you here to help avoid that?"

"Ha! Who, us?"

They're so bad at being honest. Seeing Ayla's reaction, I realized she seemed to be rooting for us to win this war. *I wonder if she talked about it with Kalen.*

"Err, um, excuse me. Could I butt in?" Porter asked, his eyes darting back and forth.

Porter appeared to be a young boy, a little on the short side, with brown hair and a pale face dotted with faint freckles. He didn't seem to suit the violent Kartinas, not at all. However, you couldn't judge Porter by his looks.

He was already well into his thirties but had been captured and experimented on by a mad sorcerer as a child, resulting in a curse that kept him from physically growing up.

"This is a report on mad sorcerers running amok once again." Porter placed a document on the table Rodrigo had set up.

It was a blank sheet of paper until he exposed it to steam. Only then did writing appear.

"So they went over to the Veloki Kingdom," Rodrigo muttered.

Is the sorcerer he had fought one of them?

"However..."

"Yes?"

"They should be under the control of the pope."

"What does that mean?" Ayla asked.

Porter cleared his throat. Though his face seemed calm as he talked about the mad sorcerers, his voice trembled momentarily. *He must be remembering what happened to him.*

"Twenty-five years ago, mad sorcerers ran amok all across the empire."

"Go on."

Ayla waved her hand dismissively, as if reacting to every statement was too bothersome. Porter looked around, searching for everyone's approval. Everyone indicated their agreement in their own ways.

"Twenty-five years ago," Porter continued. "There used to be many more sorcerers. People who could produce a flame in their hands were quite common. Sorcerers were always treated well, and people would pay handsomely for magic. But a few of the sorcerers devised an evil plan. They demanded independence. Back then, sorcerers were affiliated with their countries of origin, and their magic was restricted by law. Especially when it came to experimenting."

Porter paused for a moment to let this soak in.

Then, he continued, "Those sorcerers came together and formed a group. They called themselves the Free Dragons and fought for the freedom of research, but when you looked closer, what they really wanted was to use their magic freely, however they wanted."

It was about time for the Kartinas and their misdeeds to be mentioned. I eyed Rodrigo warily.

"They would purchase slaves and experiment on them, kill each other to gain more power, things like that." Porter skipped over the Kartinas' contributions to all of this. "At the time, the emperor and the pope declared that they would no longer turn a blind eye to the sorcerers and began to persecute them."

"How honorable of the emperor," Ada mocked.

Porter sighed. He said, "His Majesty felt threatened by their growing power, you see. The sorcerers were only useful if he could control them."

"Hmm," Ada mumbled.

"So, what happened after that?"

CHAPTER
FORTY-ONE

Jane's question hung in the air. This incident was usually not a part of the Kartina curriculum. Even the empire wasn't enthusiastic about it because the pope had taken all the credit.

"The pope had them captured. In the end, the mad sorcerers weren't punished and were simply recruited into the church."

"Why? Why weren't they killed?" Ayla snapped, like she just couldn't comprehend it. Porter smiled bitterly. He said, "That is a mystery to this day."

My turn to ask a question. "Have there been any rumors of those mad sorcerers' escape?"

Porter shrugged, explaining, "As you know, even our guild has a hard time obtaining intel on the papal court."

The papal court was the most secretive location in the empire. The sorcerer's tower was where forbidden magic users were usually controlled. However, ever since the incident with the mad sorcerers, the tower had lost all its authority.

"I see. The only thing we can do... is to go to Veloki ourselves."

Everyone turned to look at me and shook their heads.

"It's too dangerous, Estella."

"But if we do not find a way to neutralize those mad sorcerers, we won't be able to win."

"Victory is not important. I just want this war to end as quickly as possible."

Ada's words stung.

"It's important to me!"

It was. Rodrigo would be happy if we managed to help him win this war. And if my family were on favorable terms with him, perhaps he would have mercy even if he were to go berserk someday. Still, more importantly, this could stop him from going into a frenzy altogether.

The timing of the mad sorcerers' appearance was different from the novel, which meant that it could turn out differently as well. In the story, the sorcerers killed all of Rodrigo's closest subordinates. Everyone close to him. However, I couldn't remember them being related to the pope. Maybe it was because I had been living here for seventeen years already, but my memory of the plot was becoming blurry.

"I will go," Rodrigo said.

"What about the warfront?" I raised my voice before I could stop myself. I didn't want to put Rodrigo in danger.

"Devlon will take care of it." He cast a glance past me into the distance.

When I turned around to see what he was looking at, a group of knights came into sight, kicking up dust as they approached. Ada and Ayla raised their arms in front of me protectively, but I lowered their hands and returned them to their sides. Judging by Rodrigo's reaction, these knights were on our side.

"Your Grace!"

"You're late, Devlon."

"Are you all right?"

"I should be asking that."

For a moment, we stood by and watched the reunion between Devlon, who had been searching for his master, and Rodrigo, who was the cause of his worries.

"It was impossible to avoid hurting the slaves. We had to resort to digging up the ground and laying down explosives."

It was obvious what had happened after that. Jane and I frowned, holding back our reactions while Ayla and Ada let out huffs of laughter at the idea of minimizing damage.

Rodrigo turned to glower at the two of them, but they shrugged and just avoided his gaze. This wasn't time for laughter, but it made me smile to see that Rodrigo, Ada, and Ayla seemed to have become slightly closer. Jane tugged at my skirt.

"And?"

"The attacks died down at sundown. We thought you had succeeded in your attack then."

"I failed," Rodrigo said nonchalantly, but you could hear the guilt in his words.

"I see." Devlon couldn't hide his disappointment.

It wasn't directed at Rodrigo but more like sadness at the thought of having to go up against slaves once more.

I interrupted them. "It'll be over soon."

Losing hope during a war meant defeat. Without imagining a bright future, you could never live through the hellish routine of war. There would be more defectors, and this time, it would cause uncontrollable chaos.

"How so?"

I calmly explained my plan. About the mad sorcerers, and...

"I will infiltrate the Veloki Kingdom myself."

"I will go with her. So Devlon, lead the warfront for me."

"Your Grace!" Devlon's exclamation was akin to a scream.

"Porter and my sisters, Ada and Ayla, will help." I turned to Ada and Ayla.

Porter was my underling, so I had no need to ask for his permission, and he had a debt to collect from the mad sorcerers anyway. He would insist on coming even if I told him to go back.

"How about we go with you, and Rodrigo stays behind

instead?" Porter chimed in.

"No. His Grace Rodrigo has been to Veloki before, so he will be a much more suitable companion," Porter said.

At his words, Ada and Ayla narrowed their eyes. Still, he was an informant, which meant they would have to have more precise and pertinent information to counter his argument, and Ada and Ayla couldn't possibly manage that.

"Do you have a death wish?"

Instead, they raised their swords. Rodrigo pushed their blades aside with his hand.

Goosebumps shivered across my skin as Rodrigo touched those sharp blades with his bare hand without hesitation. I rubbed my arms as I moved to stand next to him.

"Stop being so reckless," I whispered.

"Are you worried about me? How nice," he teased.

I shook my head. It seemed like things were wrapping up. Ada and Ayla were huffing and puffing but unable to dispute Porter's words while Rodrigo and I stood there, waiting for their approval.

"One week." Devlon sighed as he spoke up.

"No longer than a week."

"That's too long!" Ada exclaimed in despair, but Devlon just sighed again.

One week to infiltrate the Veloki Kingdom and find useful

information. In other words, he expected us not to eat or sleep. *I didn't think Sir Devlon was this cruel...* I turned toward Rodrigo.

"All right."

"Pardon?" I blurted out.

"One week. I'll leave things to you until I return."

He took my bag from Jane and placed me on top of the horse that Devlon had ridden here. I was amazed at how easily he lifted me up, as if I weighed as little as a feather.

"There's no time, so we'll leave now. Buy us as much time as possible. We're changing strategies. Do anything you need to survive. But minimize any harm to the citizens of the empire."

Rodrigo was right. Now that a mad sorcerer had joined the fray, they could not fight while trying to protect the enemy. Rodrigo's arm came up in front of me.

"I know how to ride a horse," I told him.

"I know that."

"It would be better if we each had a horse."

"War horses are precious. Do you not know how valuable each war horse can be on the battlefield?"

"Oh..." I nodded and looked straight ahead.

For a second, I had been under the impression that Rodrigo just wanted to ride a horse with me. *It always comes up in romance novels!* Remembering that the novel I had read had not been a romance novel, I fanned my flushed face.

"Hold on tight," Rodrigo said.

I grabbed the reins. Rodrigo's taut arms and large hands were right next to me.

"Be careful, Estella! Message us anytime!" Ayla called.

She was referring to the magic paper. Since Porter was with them, they could locate me at any moment if I wrote to them. There was no better backup.

"Please do your best, Ada, Ayla!"

Hoping that the Kartinas would once again achieve great things on the battlefield, I whispered to Rodrigo, "Let's go."

Rodrigo dug his heels into the horse's side. The war horse whinnied as it galloped across the battlefield.

Entering the Veloki Kingdom was relatively easy. Many of the Velokians that Rodrigo had helped in the past assisted us. Worry scraped the back of my mind every time I thought about it. They were helping us despite the risks and the ongoing war.

"You'll have to repay them later," I said.

He smiled brightly at my comment, replying, "It was simply their turn to repay me."

He must have lived an upstanding life. I tried to remember Rodrigo's past but then shook my head. This wasn't the time to reminisce.

I asked, "Where are we going, anyway?"

"Just trust me."

It had been a while since Rodrigo had smiled so brightly. Soon, we arrived at a small house. We were able to wash up and borrow Velokian clothes to wear. Rodrigo was so tall that his shirt and pants were too short, but he really was handsome no matter what he was wearing. Still, the same applied to me.

"I see you had a good reason for declining our offer to introduce you to some pretty girls." The middle-aged man who was hosting us laughed aloud.

Rodrigo slipped an arm around my waist and pulled me closer.

He said, "Of course. There isn't anyone as pretty as my love in the whole world."

He got along well with the Velokians. It seemed as though he had known them for a long time. While we stayed among them, he even seemed more relaxed. I watched him as if I was enjoying a piece of art.

The evenings brought a chill even though it was early summer in the Veloki Peninsula in the northwest. After the sun went down and some time passed, they lit the fireplace. Then they hung a large cauldron over the fire before pouring cheap bottles of wine into it. Soon, the whole house was filled with warmth and a pleasant aroma.

Rodrigo and I sat next to each other on a couch with holes here and there as we watched our hosts move about. The sound of the wood crackling and the wine bubbling filled the air. The middle-aged couple squabbled a bit, telling each other to fetch this and that. They added some honey to the hot wine, handed us each a cup, and disappeared. We sat there peacefully, watching the flames.

"I wanted to give you only the best, but I seem to be failing," Rodrigo said.

I jolted, like someone being woken up from a deep sleep. I had no idea what he was saying.

"Pardon?"

"I wanted to give you only the best experiences."

"But why..."

CHAPTER
FORTY-TWO

For me? We were going to marry out of convenience. I knew that he was a man who did his best to fulfill every condition of a contract, but this didn't seem necessary. And more importantly, I was truly enjoying this moment. *Have I ever felt at peace like this during my seventeen years living as a Kartina?*

The Kartinas were always trying to keep me hidden. I wasn't the real Estella, so the love I received was overwhelming, and I was busy doing damage control for their misdeeds... Never once had I been able to relax, not even for a day.

Thinking about it, I resented whoever had sent me inside this body.

"That is a little disappointing," Rodrigo said as he swiveled the wine in his glass.

"What is?"

"That I seem to be the only one serious about our relationship."

"So am I."

He grimaced at my nonchalant answer, but I was serious. I wanted to survive, I wanted the Kartinas to live, and right now,

I wanted this war to end. I wished to find the female lead as soon as possible so I could hand Rodrigo off to her and quietly wait for the story to end.

Are you sure about that? From somewhere inside of me, a voice whispered.

What do you mean? I argued with it.

Do you really want to hand Rodrigo off to her and have things end that way?

Of... course. The words stuck in my throat, and I swallowed hard. A corner of my heart ached.

I looked down at my feet. The slippers our host's wife had given me to wear were far too big for me, whereas Rodrigo's slippers were too small for him. As I stared at my loose slippers and his toes sticking out from his slippers, I successfully held back the desire that threatened to rear its head.

"We should go to bed."

I finished my wine. The bitter liquid combined with the sweet honey made for an amazing drink.

"All right, let's go." Rodrigo stood up and held his hand out to me.

And a few moments later...

"Wait, this is not acceptable! I have to talk to the madam!" I exclaimed but was stopped by Rodrigo, who was blocking the door.

"We are in a relationship, and it is expected for lovers to share a room in Veloki. It would be rude to ask for an extra room when they have done so much for us already. There are only two bedrooms in this house, to begin with. Do you want to make them sleep in the living room?"

That made sense, but... I sunk in gloom.

"But there's only one bed."

Rodrigo nodded.

"There's not even a couch!" *We can't even do the "you sleep on the bed, and I'll take the couch" thing.*

"Indeed."

"Are you going to sleep on the floor?" I asked.

"I cannot."

Liar. Rodrigo had grown up on the battlefield and must have slept in ditches, never mind the ground.

"Should I sleep on the floor?"

"Why?" he asked innocently.

"Well, because we're..."

"We are going to be married, and I intend to do so. I have even told you when I will propose to you."

"Goodness, I've never even heard of a preannounced proposal!"

"I tend to do things my way."

"That's not the issue right now!"

When I talked to Rodrigo, we sometimes went off-topic, and I followed whatever meandering path he led me on.

"What is the issue, then? It's not as if we are so in love that we would die without each other. Do you think of me as a shameless beast? I apologize, but the man you will marry does not lay a finger on a woman if she's not willing." Rodrigo seemed offended.

Honestly, I was more worried about myself. Even if we were to fall asleep on either end of the bed, I tossed and turned so much in my sleep that I was bound to end up cuddled up next to him. I was used to sleeping while hugging a large pillow, but when there wasn't one available, I needed at least a rolled-up blanket...

"There's only one blanket. And only two pillows." I observed the bed. "Can I use both of the pillows?"

I grimaced at Rodrigo, resigning myself to my fate, then made puppy eyes at him. *Please?*

He chuckled. "I suppose I should let my household staff know that the archduchess's bed is to be covered in pillows. I did not know you were so fond of them," he said annoyingly before lying on the bed and pushing his pillow to my side.

The sight of his back as he turned away from me with his arm folded under his head was magnificent. I took a deep breath to calm myself down. It was true that the male lead in any story was undoubtedly attractive.

Rodrigo leaned into the bed, listening to Estella's even breathing. Was the woman with a hand on his stomach and a leg draped over his thigh really the same Estella who had made a fuss about being unable to share a bed?

He chuckled, recalling how she had turned all huffy as she commanded him not to cross the center of the bed, hugging her pillow tightly. Just as Rodrigo managed to settle his conflicted feelings and was about to fall asleep, Estella, who had fallen asleep with his pillow clutched to her like a shield, turned around and draped herself over him, practically throttling his thoughts. Rodrigo had frozen in place.

"Who exactly was she worried about?" He exhaled an exasperated laugh.

It was fortunate that they weren't given sleepwear and were dressed in their thicker day clothes. Otherwise...

"Stop."

Rodrigo shook his head. Her warm, soft breath reached his chest. His conflicted thoughts melted away. All his senses zeroed in on Estella.

His sleeves were rolled up, so her wavy hair tickled his forearms. He could smell her scent as he breathed in. Her warmth washed over him. And all he could see was her pale skin. She slept so soundly, her breathing even, that it irked him.

Disordered, brutal thoughts plagued Rodrigo. He wanted to wake her up, bite her, and devour her. His breath hitched as his thoughts' intensity startled him. He knew himself all too well. Estella had said that he was a good man, but he knew better. His true self was hideous.

Whenever he saw the lovely Estella, and whenever he faced death on the battlefield, he would regret not hugging her, pushing her down, even forcing himself onto her. His hideous greed and selfishness wanted to keep her chained to his side. To Rodrigo, the agreement they had made no longer held meaning.

But Estella does not feel the same.

His red eyes shone with desire. Just imagining her small body writhing under him made his blood boil hungrily. It would be impossible to sleep.

"Good morning!" I greeted Rodrigo brightly when he finally woke up.

I ended up sleeping in his arms, but thankfully, I was able to wake up before he did. I was relieved that he didn't seem to have noticed I had slept in his embrace. I felt light and energetic, especially because it had been a while since I had slept so well. However, the same didn't seem to apply to Rodrigo.

"Did you not sleep well?"

"I didn't." His tone was curt.

"D-did you get sleep paralysis?"

"I dreamed about being buried under a pile of rocks."

Was that because I draped my arms and legs over him? When I looked at him solemnly, he chuckled. He stood languidly, stepping closer to me as I drew open the curtains. The bright sunlight shone over him.

I guess this is when you use the word "radiant." I wondered whether leads had an instinct for knowing where to stand so the light would hit them at the perfect angle.

"Did you sleep well?" he returned the question, his tone softer.

"I did."

He exhaled a long sigh.

Are you annoyed that I'm the only one who slept well?

He mimicked me as I turned my head from side to side to stretch my neck.

"It would be best to put only one pillow in your bedroom," he said.

"Why?"

"I just think that would be best."

What does that even mean? I was about to ask him when we were called downstairs for breakfast.

"Go this way. This is as far as I can take you."

"This is more than enough."

This was as far as our middle-aged host was willing to help us. All the way to a hole in the walls of the royal palace. *Why does this hole even exist? More importantly, how does he know about it?*

"Let us go."

We hopped off our host's wagon. His eyes widened—he must've been surprised by how I jumped down without anyone's assistance. I smiled brightly and waved farewell to him. Rodrigo gently grasped my arm and pulled me along.

"There will be time for farewells after the war is over," he said, hurrying our pace.

We clambered through the hole in the wall and onto the palace grounds. What next? A secret passage. Inside it, we crawled on for a long, long time through the damp dark. Finally, we arrived at a thick door.

"This is much easier than I expected."

Rodrigo chuckled at my comment. "Let's see if it continues to be easy."

He pushed open the thick door. Someone was inside the quiet room it led into.

"Hey."

That someone gave us an awkward smile, seemingly unsurprised by our sudden appearance out of a secret door.

It was Franz, the king of Veloki.

"You... don't look good," Rodrigo said.

He must have been locked in here. Franz, the king of Veloki, was locked up in his own room. I was in disbelief. What exactly was happening in Veloki?

"I did not think it would turn out this way, either," Franz admitted.

Rodrigo and Franz spoke to each other as if they were close friends. Franz's gaze landed on me, and Rodrigo moved before me as if to hide me. He asked the king to tell him what had happened.

"It all happened in the span of four days." Franz sounded bitter as he began his account.

Four days ago, his ministers presented him with a plan to end the war with the empire.

"*The Use of Sorcerers.*" Franz exhaled an exasperated huff.

There were no sorcerers skilled enough to put an end to a war. At that moment, Blanche, one of the oldest ministers who had served three generations of Velokian kings and served as the focal point of the aristocracy, had stepped up.

"*I know of a few.*"

Blanche had asked for a private meeting, and although Franz wasn't fond of him, he trusted his loyalty, so he had allowed it. Blanche had told him about the mad sorcerers, and Franz asked for a day's time to think it over. In reality, he had never intended to agree to this plan, but he couldn't risk making an enemy of Blanche.

Franz had taken the throne by force. A lot of blood had been shed, and the factions had been divided. If they were to divide further, it could lead to the whole kingdom splitting up, so Franz had made a politically sound decision. Still, that didn't mean he would allow the mad sorcerers to join in the war.

"*If only I had someone to confide in.*"

Franz was a lonely king. There were only a few men around him whom he could truly rely on and speak to honestly. He had gathered them and taken the day to discuss the issue at hand. Their conclusion was the same. Sorcerers were calculating. They couldn't possibly predict what they would demand in return for helping with the war.

"*I reject this plan.*"

Just as he had declared his decision, the mad sorcerers barged in. Their presence alone was enough for the hair on the back of Franz's neck to stand on end. They were so monstrously deformed that you could hardly call them human. However, they weren't monsters, either. They could speak and act like regular people, and their eyes were unmistakably human.

"Accept our assistance."

The sorcerers had threatened him, and Franz's advisors had risen in anger. Blood had spilled in the king's reception room.

"Your reception room seems to be full of insects. Their words are annoying."

All he could do was tell them to wait. It was now the fourth day since Franz had been locked in his own room. It seemed Blanche had been taking care of the kingdom's affairs during this time.

"I see. That's why I couldn't reach you."

"Yes. But how did you get in here?"

As soon as he had us sit on the couch, Franz moved to the door and pressed his ear against it to try and detect if anyone was outside. Fortunately, the hallway seemed empty because he quickly returned to sit across from us.

CHAPTER
FORTY-THREE

"I got help from my lover." Rodrigo gestured at me.

Well, we got help from the Mave Guild, to be exact. After we had come through the hole in the palace walls, we had taken a moment to contemplate our next move. Then, I remembered something. That there was a secret passageway into the palace. Rodrigo had considered my words for a moment before immediately finding the first entrance.

"How did you know where it was?"

"The imperial palace has a similar secret passage."

Oh, right, Rodrigo is the archduke. Seeing Rodrigo in a new light, I had followed him. It had been easy after that... until we reached a dead end. I then had to send a message to Porter via magic paper in an attempt to grasp at straws, and he replied immediately.

"Keep going left. The first king loved anything 'left.'"

That hint had led us to King Franz.

"Your lover?" Franz looked at me.

Only then did Rodrigo step aside to allow him to see me.

"I have urgent business to discuss with you."

He's not even going to introduce me?

At Rodrigo's words, Franz turned his gaze from me.

"Is it related to the war?"

"The sorcerers."

Franz groaned and put his hand on his forehead. "So they joined the battle."

"You didn't know?"

Franz clenched his fists. It was enough of an answer. Rodrigo and I exchanged glances, our heads tilted to one side.

"So, this is a rebellion," Rodrigo concluded after listening to everything that had happened in the palace recently.

"You're being treated very kindly, considering that." I gestured around us.

There was not even a speck of dust in Franz's room. An array of expensive-looking snacks lay untouched nearby. Steam rose from a kettle that must have been brought in recently.

"It's hard to explain, but I am still the king," Franz said.

This was a common occurrence. King Franz did not have a solid support base. His opposition had neutralized him politically, keeping the rebellion's impact in mind. Just enough to keep control. *It comes up a lot in novels, right?*

"I understand. Is there anyone who can help you?"

Rodrigo's lips parted in awe as if he was surprised at what I had said.

"You understand this situation?" he asked.

I knew right away that he wasn't simply referring to the situation at hand. People communicated with body language and subtle looks other than just words, after all. Rodrigo was surprised that I had grasped everything just by looking at the short-term outcome. *He really underestimates me, doesn't he?*

I called him out on it, "Are you underestimating me, Rodrigo?"

Rodrigo frowned. "Of course not. I'm just impressed by my lover's talents."

Hmph, so that's what you're going with? Fine, I'll let it go. This isn't important right now.

"I feel as though the both of you really do understand my situation."

Unlike other royals, Franz was incredibly humble. Perhaps it was because he had been persecuted so much since childhood. It was nice to see a royal who wasn't boastful.

"Unfortunately, anyone willing to help me is being kept locked up as well."

"They have no legitimate reason to keep them locked away, do they? Besides, we were prepared for this."

We were?

When I looked at Rodrigo with wide eyes, he smiled awkwardly and whispered, "Later."

"Oh, their confinement is not official. They simply cannot leave their place. Sorcerers are keeping watch over them. And what we had prepared... unfortunately, my confinement put an end to it."

Finally, we got to the topic we were here to discuss. It felt like we had taken the long way around.

"Ha... You must have had a hard time. But why are they here? Did your kingdom decide to take in those madmen?"

Franz shook his head.

"Do you know about the mad sorcerers?" Rodrigo asked.

"Vaguely," Franz replied.

"Your Majesty, if you decide to take them in, it would be turning the entire continent against you. Are you aware of this? It wouldn't just be the Philemon Empire. Are you not aware that the Western Empire is also on the same page as our empire when it comes to the mad sorcerers?"

"I am aware of that. That is why I was against this, but..." Franz pressed his lips together.

For the first time, I could see the fury in his eyes.

"There is someone who has sided with them."

"Who?"

"Blanche."

"Kill him."

"Ha!" Franz laughed at Rodrigo's simple advice. He said,

"Sir Rodrigo, I really like you. Your strength, your brilliant mind, your wealth... But even you cannot have everything you want, isn't that right? I know very well that you are persecuted in your own land. You should know that you cannot win every battle just because you have power."

That meant that he couldn't fight Blanche.

"What is the reason?"

I couldn't understand Franz.

"I am the king. Blanche is the center of the aristocracy. Removing him would mean turning all of the nobles against me."

"Even if he committed a great crime? Even if he was hated by them?"

"Unfortunately, there is no hard evidence against him, and he has no enemies among the nobles because he is benevolent to those on his side."

I grinned. I had seen many cases in which people who had been allies in the morning had turned their backs on each other by night. *I wonder if those nobles who pretend to be allies would stand up for each other when push came to shove. Of course not. And...*

"The reason Blanche was able to recruit the mad sorcerers is because he isn't the one taking responsibility for it." I glanced between Franz and Rodrigo, ensuring I had their attention before I continued. "If we let him be, he will end up getting credit for having put a quick end to the war. Both the nobles and the citizens are unhappy about the war dragging on. Whatever the means, Blanche will gain the accolade of putting an end to the war. His influence in the kingdom will increase. Your Majesty, on the other hand, will be held responsible for bringing the mad sorcerers into the war. The other nations will not let it go. The kingdom's reputation will tank, and trade will begin to dry out."

This would never happen in the twenty-first century. However, it was possible in this novel's setting. Here, reputation was more important than economic gain.

"Is that what he's after?" Rodrigo muttered beside me.

I nodded before looking at Franz. "We have to make sure he is held responsible for all of this."

"How?"

"You should step down." I smiled so widely that my eyes turned into a crescent shape. I told them plainly, "Hand over the throne to Blanche."

Franz and Rodrigo flinched.

Wait, what's with this reaction? I perked an eyebrow at them.

A sound at the door quieted our conversation. Someone was coming into the room. Rodrigo and I had to return to the secret passage hidden next to the fireplace.

"I will put whatever is necessary in there. You will come again, will you not?" Franz whispered urgently.

I looked over at Rodrigo. "We must meet at least once more, don't you think?"

Franz looked relieved as he closed the entrance.

The secret passage was enveloped in darkness. As Rodrigo muttered something and snapped his fingers, a small flame appeared above his palm. A warm light illuminated the passage.

"Magic is so convenient."

Rodrigo smiled at my reaction.

"What?"

"Most people get really excited when they see magic. You seem far too nonchalant."

"Oh, is that what you want? Wow, it's so cool! How amazing! Like that?"

Rodrigo grimaced at my overenthusiastic acting and shook his head.

"Let's just act normally."

We looked at each other before bursting into laughter.

"Look at us. We're so carefree." We were joking during a war in the middle of the enemy's territory. "I have to let Ayla and Ada know what we found out."

I retrieved another sheet of magic paper from the pack on

Rodrigo's back. There were only five sheets left now.

"You must use them wisely," Rodrigo said.

I agreed with him, saying, "Let's get back before I use them all."

I fished my hand out of his grip.

"What must we do next?" Rodrigo asked after I had sent the message.

We sat with our backs against the cold wall. Thanks to Rodrigo taking off his vest and setting it down for me, my rear wasn't cold. He was extremely apologetic even as he offered me his vest, mumbling something about wanting to give me good experiences as he had before.

"No matter how many times I think about it, this doesn't seem like a scheme dreamed up by a regular noble. Is he very ambitious?"

Rodrigo shook his head. "I met him once. When I was trying to get a business license."

Rodrigo went quiet for a moment, apparently recalling his meeting with Blanche.

"What was he like?" I asked.

"He seemed extremely greedy but also very fearful."

"What?"

"This was around the time the crown prince was abusing his power. Blanche was aware of the fact that the crown prince would not make a very good king. But he didn't talk to the king about it because he knew it would cause him harm. Though he knew the right thing to do, he did not make a move for fear of retaliation. He puts his own safety above all else."

"And he wants to make as much money as possible."

"Of course. The more money, the better."

That's an eternal truth. I nodded enthusiastically.

"After hearing your description of him, it's even more clear."

"What do you mean?"

"There is definitely someone controlling him."

"And we must find out who that is."

"Wow, we're really in sync." I held up my hand.

He looked back and forth between my face and my palm.

"You're supposed to clap your hand against mine when I hold it out like this."

I took Rodrigo's hand, which wasn't holding the magic flame, unfolded it, and pushed it against my palm.

"No, not like that!"

Although I was going for a high five, he knotted his fingers with mine.

"I prefer this if you are trying to compliment me."

I pressed my lips together at the way his voice suddenly turned serious. The flame's light flickered in his red eyes. I couldn't face them for very long.

After I wrote another message telling Porter to dig up information on Blanche, we left the secret passage. Blending seamlessly into the crowds milling into and out of the palace, we made our way across the grounds out into the city. We headed downtown, but not to Blanche Manor.

"Where are we going?"

Rodrigo strode along confidently like someone familiar with the streets of Veloki. Our hands were still intertwined. We walked along, looking to any passerby like a sweet newlywed couple.

"We are going to a place where information is cheap."

After weaving through narrower and narrower streets, we turned this way and that through a maze of alleyways. At last, we stopped in front of a small, decrepit inn.

"Is this place even open?"

Even the sign in front was lopsided and in disrepair.

"Probably," he replied, not sounding particularly confident.

"You rat bastard! You ought to pay with your body if you got no money!"

The door opened, and along with the husky voice, a young man came hurtling outside, holding his pants up haphazardly as he was chased by a middle-aged woman wielding a ladle like a sword.

"I'll bring you the money! Please, come on! Put your clothes back on!" the young man shouted as he ran for it.

Only then did I catch a good look at the woman wielding a ladle. One of her breasts was hanging out of her half-unbuttoned top.

"What are you staring at?"

I looked away at her rough voice. At the same time, I elbowed Rodrigo sharply.

"It's been a while, Beatrice."

It was an incredibly noble-sounding name, and it did not suit this rundown inn, her raspy voice, or her provocative appearance.

Wait, he knows her? When I turned to look at him, Rodrigo slipped his hand from mine and enveloped me in a hug.

"Didn't you say that once I found a lover, you wanted to meet her?" he said to Beatrice.

CHAPTER
FORTY-FOUR

Beatrice. I remained silent as she kicked out all her patrons and prepared food for us.

"She is like family to me."

Rodrigo seemed to think I had misunderstood his relationship with her because he kept telling me about her, emphasizing that they were like family. I didn't say anything. I knew very well that there was nothing going on between them, or rather, that they were just close friends. I remembered Beatrice from the novel.

"Estella."

Just as he was about to say something else, Beatrice returned. She presented us with simple bowls of soup and stale bread.

Placing a chipped beer glass in front of herself, she asked with little enthusiasm, "She's your lover?"

"Yes, for now."

"For now? Are you planning on breaking up?" she asked, sounding rather hopeful.

"Of course not, Beatrice. I'm going to marry her." Rodrigo

raised our entwined hands as if to emphasize his point.

He was acting a little weird. Usually, he was relatively calm and collected. However, in front of Beatrice, he was acting like a young boy. Probably because he was in the presence of someone who had saved his life when he was a kid.

In her youth, Beatrice was one of the women selling their bodies in war camps. She came across Rodrigo one day and saved his life. Feeling sorry for the child soldier, she gave him food and warm gloves in the winter. When the child soldier grew up and became chief, he helped her become a merchant handling supplies for the army. And after the war, she was able to settle down in Veloki.

Rodrigo had countless connections like that. As tough as his life had been, he had received help from many people and helped countless others as well. So, that wasn't the reason I still remembered her from the novel. The reason I remembered Beatrice was because she was the one who introduced Rodrigo to the female lead.

Come to think of it, wasn't she from Veloki? My memory of the novel had become blurry.

"Marriage at such a young age? Don't do anything to throw away your future." Beatrice gulped down the frothy ale.

It looked refreshing, but I was sure that in a place where ice was hard to come by, her beer was lukewarm at best.

"Why did you come here? I thought you were doing well."

Rodrigo grinned as he gobbled down her food, clearly enjoying the taste.

"Because I'm curious about the Blanche family."

Beatrice's gaze wavered for a moment. *Oh... I guess the female lead is a Blanche family member.*

"What? Why?" She rummaged through her pockets and retrieved a cigarette. It looked like she had been chewing its end.

"Why don't you just buy chewing tobacco?" Rodrigo reprimanded her further about smoking being a bad habit. He sipped his water. "Estella, does the food not suit your taste? She may look like that, but her food is quite good."

Rodrigo sounded worried. Only then did I realize I hadn't even touched the food Beatrice had brought us. It was extremely rude of me.

"I'll eat."

"Don't bother if you don't want to. Do you think I poisoned it or something? Where did you find this girl?"

I couldn't find it in me to respond to Beatrice's harsh comment. From the moment I realized who she was, my mind was all jumbled up.

"Stop it, Beatrice."

"Stop what? Find someone who suits you better. A woman who sits around elegantly drinking tea doesn't suit you at all.

Hey, miss. This bastard is actually—"

Bang.

Rodrigo slammed down his cup. Both Beatrice and I blinked at him, startled.

"That's enough, Beatrice. Do not make me regret my decision to visit an old friend." He took my hand in his and helped me up.

"Rodrigo?" I asked.

"I apologize."

His apology implied a lot. Still, I had no intention of trying to comprehend his feelings.

Instead, I said, "If there is any information to be found, we need it. I'm just feeling a little unwell. I want to get some fresh air."

I dragged Rodrigo in the opposite direction. He made no effort to stop me.

"I'll be back."

When I let go of his hand and stood up, Rodrigo tried to follow me. I pushed down on his shoulder.

"Don't worry. You know me." *I can take care of myself.* I said those words and left Rodrigo behind.

I caught sight of him roughly running his fingers through his hair in frustration as I left, but I didn't want to pay him any more mind.

The back alley was quiet. I walked carefully, avoiding the filth that littered the ground. There was no fresh air to breathe in, and it seemed like all I would get was a nose full of rancid garbage stench. Just as in any other city, beggars were hunched over in a corner, looking too much like trash bags in their rags. Discarded, rejected from society. They shot glances in my direction and raised their hands—but they didn't look like they expected much.

I was dressed as a commoner. I rummaged through my pockets. There was... nothing I could give them. I did have a few gold coins but giving them gold coins was akin to sentencing them to death as they would fight over the coins tooth and nail. I wondered what might be suitable when I remembered the bread I had left behind at Beatrice's inn.

Beatrice would probably be enraged if she found out I intended to give her bread to the beggars. She would think I was looking down at her food. However, I wasn't being picky before. Even now, I wasn't trying to disregard her hospitality.

"Ooh, lady."

The beggars suddenly became noisy. Though they had been glued to the planks they were sitting on, they suddenly stood up and moved as one. Naturally, my gaze followed them.

A woman was standing at the end of the alley. Her disposition was noble and elegant, and her face was beautiful,

benevolent. It was the heroine I had killed. Anneheine
Blanche.

"Oh, Anneheine! Come on in." Beatrice's face lit up as she
greeted Anneheine warmly.

I was completely disregarded as I followed her inside.
Still, it didn't bother me. This was meant to happen. Since
the heroine had appeared, it was only logical for everyone's
attention to move to her.

"Are you feeling better?"

But why is he still paying attention to me? Rodrigo came
closer.

"I'm f—"

Before I could finish my answer, Beatrice pushed
Anneheine in front of Rodrigo.

"Rodrigo! This is the Blanche lady I was talking about."

I guess they talked about her while I was gone.

"Introduce yourself, Anneheine! This is the young man
I kept telling you about who saved my miserable life!" Her
description seemed a bit strange.

Standing in front of Rodrigo, Anneheine blinked in
confusion. She was gorgeous but apparently nervous.

She managed, "M-My name is Anneheine Blanche."

"I am Rodrigo Duveli Erhart," he greeted her like a gentleman.

"What are you waiting for? Give him your hand!"

As they stood there awkwardly, Beatrice poked Anneheine in the back.

"Pardon? My hand?" Anneheine asked.

"That's what they do in the empire! Men greet women by kissing the back of their hands. Right, Rodrigo?" Beatrice sounded incredibly enthusiastic.

"It depends on the circumstances."

He immediately indicated his disinterest in participating and turned his whole body toward me.

"It would be best to head back today. Beatrice has a visitor."

"She seems to be your guest too. Beatrice, I would like to rest. Do you have any rooms?" I answered him coldly before approaching Beatrice.

Her gaze was chilling as she looked at me. *Oh my, it's as if she knows which family I'm from.* Her eyes were reproaching me for being greedy, like I was to blame for Rodrigo's lifelong hardships. She couldn't have known, but it felt like she did.

"There is a room upstairs, but it probably wouldn't suit your tastes... My Lady?"

She obviously can't bring herself to be polite to someone she doesn't like. I thought that if she had met me before she met

Rodrigo, we could have become friends.

"I don't mind. It'll only be for a short while."

"Then I'll also…" Rodrigo tried to follow me.

I turned to look at him, stopping in my tracks. "I want to rest alone."

You should get to know Anneheine, Rodrigo. She seemed to have fallen for him already. She looked like a girl in love, with her cheeks flushed.

"Let us leave if you are not feeling well, Estella," Rodrigo prompted.

"Do we have anywhere to go?" I asked. "Don't forget what we came here to do. This is a great opportunity, so don't squander it."

I tipped my head, just slightly, toward Anneheine. We were here to find out about the Blanche family. And a daughter of the Blanche family had appeared before us. What better informant could there be? Rodrigo's gaze was full of unspoken complaints, but he didn't stop me as I walked upstairs.

It was almost over now. If I could hand him over to the heroine before our planned marriage, it would be even better. Neither he nor I would have to go through the trouble of signing divorce papers.

I lay down on the bed, relieved. Completely relieved.

A squeaking sound irked me. *Why doesn't she get better beds?*

I thought, closing my eyes.

Another squeak.

I didn't move, though... Something's off.

I opened my eyes. I had to scream, but I couldn't. A sorcerer with only one nostril covered my mouth forcefully.

Rodrigo's attention was directed upstairs. Estella had acted strangely ever since they had met up with Beatrice. Estella's usual bright disposition had been replaced with gloom.

He had worried that she might have misunderstood his relationship with Beatrice and had tried to tell her, but she seemed entirely uninterested. And after she had returned from her walk, she had turned completely cold toward him. *Did I do something wrong?*

"I hear you want to know about my family?"

A clear voice brought Rodrigo's train of thought to a halt. It was feminine, gentle, but unlike Estella's voice, it somehow didn't capture his attention. Rodrigo looked at the woman in front of him. She was pretty. There was no exaggeration in Beatrice's praise of her that he had heard before her arrival.

Beatrice had begun to talk about this woman when he mentioned wanting information on the Blanche family. He wondered how Beatrice, who was not very fond of nobles, had befriended this woman. Still, his curiosity died down.

"Yes, I do, but I do not believe you can help me." Rodrigo politely kept her at arm's length.

"Why not?" Anneheine asked.

"Because I am looking for information on Duke Blanche's schemes."

At this point, most nobles would have become enraged, saying that he was insulting their family name, or would have tried to convince him otherwise, saying it was all a misunderstanding. She did neither.

"I'll cooperate."

Rodrigo's eyes narrowed.

"I said," she clarified. "I will help you uncover the misdeeds committed by my family."   Her clearly enunciated words were full of certainty, as if she were saying, "I know how terrible my family is."

For some reason, it reminded him of Estella. The woman who was helping him and who was trying to save him even though it would harm her family. Even with Anneheine standing before him, Rodrigo's mind was filled with thoughts about Estella.

"Your name is Rodrigo, right?"

"Pardon me, but would you please address me correctly?"

Being on a first-name basis was reserved for those close to

him. A lover like Estella, an old friend like Beatrice, a family member, or a comrade.

"Oh, right... You felt like a close friend because I've heard so much about you from Beatrice. I apologize, Sir Rodrigo."

"That's all right, Lady Blanche."

A loud noise erupted from upstairs, and Rodrigo sprang to his feet.

"Excuse me," he said, racing toward the stairs.

"I'll go!" Beatrice tried to stop Rodrigo.

However, he jumped up the stairs without paying her any attention. There weren't any other guests upstairs besides Estella. Something awful had caused such a sound. He climbed the stairs faster, racing down the hall, a terrible feeling in his gut.

CHAPTER
FORTY-FIVE

Oh shit, shit, shit!

Estella cursed inwardly.

Why is this happening? Getting kidnapped, locked up somewhere, and other unknown misfortunes were practically patented by novel heroines.

I'm just a villain! I'm supposed to be doing the kidnapping, not the other way around!

I could yell all I wanted inwardly, but I couldn't make a sound. My body was tossed to and fro. These bastards either didn't know how to use a carriage or didn't need even one because they were carrying me on their backs as they ran.

Nausea crept from my stomach up into my throat from the bumpy ride. I hung upside down from their shoulders. Great. Kidnapped and nauseated. I hadn't even felt sick the first time I had taken a portal. I pressed my lips together and closed my eyes. When I stopped struggling, the arms over my thighs loosened slightly.

What, did they think I would try to run? Ridiculous. When I realized I was up against mad sorcerers, I gave up on running away. Had they been assassins, I would have disposed of them easily. However, sorcerers were a different matter.

Even a master swordsman would have a hard time defeating them. I had to wait for the right moment.

I felt for the vial of poison in my pocket. It would allow me one chance to escape. There. A sense of relief washed away some of the nausea when I touched my fingers to the bottle's shape. At least I had something. Rodrigo had wanted me not to wear a longsword as it would attract attention. I had agreed with him. And the rest of my weapons were left behind in my bag.

It wasn't as though I could ask my kidnappers to wait for a moment while I got my bag, so all I had left was this vial of poison that I kept on me for emergencies. Therefore, I had no intention of fighting them. I didn't intend to run, either. The reason I had struggled earlier was to get more comfortable.

They ran without even stopping to take a breath, carrying me all the way. The rumor that the mad sorcerers had modified their bodies must've been true. He carried me onward for miles and miles. His breathing never even grew labored.

They let me down on the floor. And then they disappeared.

I only opened my eyes after I was sure they were gone. I had expected them to take me to a cave or some other scary place. Instead, they had brought me to a noble's room. The furniture was sleek and luxurious, and I was seated on a plush couch.

"This is so much nicer than Beatrice's inn."

I had to laugh. *How did I end up in a nicer place after getting kidnapped?*

I stood to get a better look around the room. First, I pressed my ear against the door. It was quiet, but there were muffled footsteps. Five people were in the hallway.

"I could have handled them if they weren't sorcerers."

I gave up on escaping this way—it was a bad idea, even if one of them was a sorcerer.

I headed toward the window, noting to myself, "It seems to be about the fourth floor..."

A four-story mansion. That meant whoever owned this building was quite affluent. Escaping through the window was possible, but the problem was that it was broad daylight. The likelihood of climbing down the building's walls undetected was extremely low.

I'll have to wait.

I sat on the plush couch, waiting for my kidnapper to arrive. My body was worn from being jostled, and I sank deeper and deeper into the cushions... And fell asleep.

"...Amazing."

I opened my eyes at the sound of an unfamiliar voice.

"What kind of person falls asleep so peacefully when kidnapped?" The man looking down at me sneered.

I rubbed my eyes and sat up properly.

"Hello, kidnapper. My name is Estella Kartina. Now, go ahead and tell me what you want."

I yawned widely as I watched the man's face contort with disgust and surprise. I had decided not to hide my identity now that I had been kidnapped. The Kartina family name was well-known across the entire continent.

If he knows my family, at least he will know that he can't mess with me. I glared at him, my head held high.

"Beatrice!" Rodrigo shouted, venom in his eyes.

She shook her head, her face pale.

"I-I didn't know. I-I just..."

"If anything happens to Estella, I won't be able to forgive you. Where did she go?" A vein pulsed in Rodrigo's hand as he gripped his sword too tightly.

"Please do not blame her, Sir Rodrigo." Anneheine stepped forward.

"Stay out of this."

"How could I? When it looks as though my father is the one

who kidnapped this lady named Estella," she said.

Rodrigo's eyes narrowed dangerously.

"Oh, so you're Sir Blanche."

When I revealed my identity, so did the man. He knew just as well as I did that hiding his identity would lead us nowhere.

"I have arrested you for spying."

"This looks like a very private jail cell for an official arrest."

Blanche smiled at my remark. "We do not wish to turn the Kartinas against us. We would like to continue getting supplies from your family as we do now."

Supplies from the Kartinas? I remembered the specialty thread I had handed over to the emperor. *So Blanche must be the one who bought Kartina products and brought them to Veloki.*

"So, you must return peacefully to the empire. I do not want a fight." The scrawny man sounded annoyed.

My unplanned appearance was frustrating him.

Who cares.

"Would you like me to thank you for letting me go? You could have just asked politely, don't you think?"

"Oh my, I seemed to have offended you. But I had no choice. I cannot host a spy as if they were an honored guest, can I?" He laughed.

I considered laughing along with this forced sound but decided against it. I felt bad for Rodrigo, but I decided to return to the empire like Blanche said. It was the best course of action. *I'm sure Rodrigo will take care of the rest.*

Considering they had only kidnapped me, I figured they hadn't found out about Rodrigo yet. *Keep yourself well-hidden and get back safe.*

"Let us go."

"Sure."

Still, I, no, we could not leave the room.

Bang!

With a thunderous noise, the door disappeared. As thick smoke permeated the air, someone stepped inside.

Rodrigo. He scanned the room, his eyes menacing and, at the same time, desperate. Then he found me.

Our eyes met for a moment. His gaze was gentle, but it gave me chills. He was furious.

"Aaah! P-please have mercy!" Blanche's feet dangled in the air as Rodrigo held him by the neck.

His lips twisted into a smirk. "Do you want to live?"

His usual elegant, polite tone had become cold and informal. I stood back as I watched. He didn't seem like himself.

"Sir Blanche, perhaps you deserve praise for getting me this riled up. Even His Majesty the Emperor has never managed to annoy me this much." Rodrigo ran a hand through his hair, which had fallen into his face.

The blood on his hand smeared onto his cheek and forehead. Rodrigo tossed Blanche onto the ground with an expression that suited the crimson.

"Argh!" Blanche writhed on the ground, shouting in pain.

He retrieved a small bell from his inside pocket and began to shake it vigorously. He was calling for backup. I threw a teacup that sat next to me, aiming for his wrist.

"Ugh!"

The bell clattered to the floor. Blanche glowered over at me for throwing the teacup at him, but he couldn't face me for long. Rodrigo started kicking his face.

"There are more people coming, Rodrigo. Let's go."

I grabbed Rodrigo's arm at the sound of footsteps in the distance. Slowly, he turned to me. His red eyes glinted with fury.

"Get a hold of yourself, Rodrigo. We have a goal to achieve."

We had to find out the relationship between Blanche and the mad sorcerers.

"It appears to be too late to go about this politely. So..."

"Do you have a plan?"

"I plan on killing them all first." Rodrigo lightly pushed me aside and moved in front of me.

Two mad sorcerers and many knights burst into the room.

"I suppose it is too late to stop him?" A small, frail voice rang out.

It was Anneheine. I had wondered how Rodrigo had made it all the way here without being caught, but this explained it. *Is it also because of her that he's gone mad?*

"It's too late." I had to agree with her.

One of the mad sorcerers swung at Rodrigo with sharp claws. The fight had begun. I left Blanche with Anneheine.

"You'll die if you run."

This was a threat.

"I won't."

The way Anneheine was treating her father did not seem familial. Why? However, I had to trust her. In the novel, she would do anything and everything for Rodrigo. I figured that the changed circumstances didn't necessarily mean that her basic character traits had changed.

"Don't run. I'm serious," I told her once more before ripping a slit down my skirt.

"What are you doing?" Anneheine's eyes widened, her voice rising as I threw off my shoes as well.

"Even Rodrigo will get exhausted eventually. That will

make him vulnerable. I have no intention of letting him get hurt." I smiled at Anneheine and then jumped into the fray.

The room was large, but it felt cramped, with everyone rushing in. Though they must have been aware that it was dangerous to swing a sword in tight spaces, the knights didn't hold back.

Idiots. I clicked my tongue and kicked one of the knights injured by an ally's blade. Taking the opportunity as he staggered at the sudden attack, I twisted his wrist. He lost his grip on his sword.

"Thank you. I'll get good use out of this."

I had heard that this family was rich, and the quality of the knight's sword affirmed it. It would be plenty suitable for this fight. Readjusting my grip on the sword, I left Rodrigo to deal with the mad sorcerers and began to cut down the knights one by one.

"What are you all doing? You can't even defeat one woman?" the knights began to shout at each other.

"The man is our target! Get rid of her quickly and support the others!" a man yelled as he passed me and headed for Rodrigo. He seemed to have a higher rank.

You're first! I spun around and thrust my sword at him. It was such a quick movement that my blonde hair spun around and whipped me in the face. The man managed to twist his body and avoid being stabbed in the stomach, but the sword pierced his side.

"Argh!" He stepped back with a short shout of pain, cradling his ribs.

"Go ahead and try to get past me." I smiled as I swung my sword at the man's wrist.

He toppled onto the ground, getting in the way of his comrades, and a few tripped over him. I laughed. The knights' expressions were a sight to see. They had clearly underestimated me because I was a woman.

"Did I mention that I'm a Kartina?"

The knights all grimaced at this revelation.

"Don't go easy on her because she's a woman! She's a Kartina!"

Even knights of a different kingdom were familiar with the Kartinas' notoriety. I felt much better knowing that they would now rush at me with all their strength. They wouldn't be able to claim that they had gone easy on me because I was a woman. I turned to shoot a glance at Rodrigo, who was fighting valiantly.

Will he be able to handle two mad sorcerers? His magic hasn't awakened completely yet.

My heart began to beat faster. It was an unpleasant feeling fueled by anxiety and concern.

I have to hurry up and get to him. If things got down to it... I would have to make a choice.

Is it right for me to save Rodrigo if that happens? No, stop being so pessimistic.

Facing the five blades swinging my way, I dismissed any errant thoughts.

CHAPTER
FORTY-SIX

"Ha..."

Rodrigo's vision was becoming blurry. He could still see Estella swinging her sword, but everything was beginning to blacken at the edges. He strained his eyes, trying to clear his head. He staggered, trying to catch himself, and a sorcerer brandished claw-like fingernails at him, shooting a burst of fire magic in his direction.

"We're indoors, you idiot!" Rodrigo cursed as he raised a wall of ice.

It melted instantly into a cloud of steam as the fire magic made contact with it. He took advantage of everyone's obscured sight to snatch a sword from the floor and cast a magical aura over it. There were many restrictions to using magic in a confined space, but he was out of mana.

If I use more magic, I may not survive.

He could feel it. He had no choice but to use his physical strength. The mad sorcerers were still human. If he was exhausted, they had to be too.

Two, maybe three more?

Rodrigo hesitated mid-thought as he counted the number of magic casts he had left because one of the sorcerers he had knocked out temporarily had shot more magic at him. Rodrigo sent the sword soaring, its blade covered in a magical aura.

"Aaargh!"

"Oh."

He hadn't meant to kill him.

Because the sorcerer started to run to avoid his sword, it stabbed straight through his heart. The sorcerer collapsed, clutching his chest. There was no time for any last words. At the sight of his comrade's death, the other sorcerer turned to run.

Capturing someone who had lost the will to fight was easy. Rodrigo grabbed the back of the mad sorcerer's collar before he could get very far. The man struggled but, after a minute or two, held still.

"Are you swooping in to steal my kill?"

"I'm helping you."

Estella, who had managed to defeat all the knights, pointed her sword at the mad sorcerer's heart. He stopped resisting.

"Wouldn't it be better to put cloth in his mouth so he doesn't bite his tongue, Rodrigo?"

"He won't kill himself. It would be better to cut off his hands so he can't use any more magic."

With the mad sorcerer between them, Rodrigo and Estella burst out laughing. What an awfully unsuitable conversation for lovers.

They said a crisis was an opportunity. *When I got kidnapped, I assumed I would have to return to the empire without much success, but...* I looked down at Blanche and the mad sorcerer kneeling before me.

"Your name?"

We couldn't just keep calling him a mad sorcerer.

"Vandula."

Though his features were grotesquely modified, his voice sounded normal. Just as Rodrigo had said, he didn't seem eager to kill himself.

"Why did you kidnap me?" I demanded.

"Because we heard you were investigating us."

"And how did you know about that?"

"We have eyes and ears."

It seemed that there had been magical devices hidden in Franz's room. Rodrigo straightened up, clearly annoyed at this revelation. He spot-cleaned the blood that had sprayed onto his clothes before chucking the red-soaked towel onto the floor. Blanche and Vandula winced.

They're ridiculous. I thought I was pretty scary myself, but they're clearly not intimidated by me. I blamed my kind-looking face, suddenly feeling grumpy.

"If you are feeling unwell, you should rest for a moment, Estella," Rodrigo said.

He must've interpreted my furrowed eyebrows as a sign of fatigue.

"I'm fine, Rodrigo. Let's wrap this up quickly and leave."

Blanche and Vandula grew pale at the lack of emotion in my voice.

"I'm sorry, but... may I speak?"

It was Anneheine. She was sitting comfortably on the couch, even with her father on his knees.

What is up with those two? For a moment, I was curious about her relationship with her family, but I soon stopped caring. In the end, it had nothing to do with me. However, it might matter to Rodrigo.

"What will be my father's punishment?"

"What did you say?" Rodrigo asked.

"Losing his title, execution, imprisonment, or... hm, maybe exile? I'm asking what his punishment will be."

Rodrigo seemed at a loss for words for a moment. I felt the same. It sounded as though Anneheine wanted her father to be punished.

"Hm, I am not sure. We cannot punish him ourselves."

"Why not? My father kidnapped you and even tried to kill you."

"We are not from here, and we aren't here on an official visit, either."

If Blanche claimed that he had kidnapped and imprisoned us for spying, that would be it.

"Ha... That's no good."

Anneheine looked unwell.

"Miss Anneheine?"

When I called her name, she raised her head.

She was biting her lip, looking very much troubled.

She said, "Take me with you, then."

She took a firm hold of my hand, causing Rodrigo's eyebrows to furrow. Blanche seemed unaffected by his daughter's betrayal. As if he had expected this to happen. Or as if this had happened before.

"Miss Anneheine, I thank you for leading Rodrigo here, but—"

"Then take me with you."

I had read that she was a calm, quiet person, but this was pretty aggressive.

"That's enough, Lady Anneheine. We do not know what issues you have with Blanche, but to Estella and I, you are simply his daughter."

"I'm not his daughter! We don't share a single drop of blood!" Anneheine cried out. Her trembling hands gestured toward Blanche. "I am not that man's daughter! He simply brought me here to play doll!"

At the mention of "playing doll," the novel's pages I had forgotten were restored. Blanche was a pervert.

Oh, right... That man is absolute garbage. He found pleasure in dressing up cute, lovely girls in pretty dresses. And then, once the girls became adults... *R-rated vulgarity. The author is such trash...*

I stopped trying to remember more.

"You are my daughter, Anneheine. Stop denying it."

He sounded so benevolent. Blanche was right. She was, in fact, his real daughter. He was actually impotent. However, just once, he had used magic to be able to impregnate a woman, and Anneheine was the result. It made me understand why he had joined forces with the sorcerers.

"No, I'm not your daughter!" Tears streamed down Anneheine's face, and she clung to my arm. "Please take me with you. I beg of you."

"We cannot," Rodrigo answered in my stead.

I shivered at how cold he sounded.

"We do have much to thank you for, but we do not wish to

have any ties with Blanche." Rodrigo's words were effective.

Anneheine's hand slid away from my arm. "What will happen to me then?"

"It appears that your father does not intend to punish you."

Blanche hadn't raised his voice or become angry even once after Anneheine had appeared. *I guess he loves her enough to turn a blind eye to her betrayal. That would be a redeeming quality if he weren't a pervert. And a villain, kind of like my own father.*

My heart ached as I thought of Stefan. *Does he have any idea what I'm going through? I guess he wouldn't just sit back if he did.* Getting kidnapped by a Velokian might have been the fastest way to end this war.

"Estella, could you watch Blanche? I must talk to the sorcerer in private."

I was very curious about what that conversation would entail, but I agreed to his request since I couldn't interrogate a sorcerer myself.

"All right, Rodrigo. And don't forget that we only have two days left."

"Of course. We wouldn't want the Kartinas to march over here with their army."

Maybe we do want that. I chuckled and snapped my fingers at Blanche.

"What is your bedroom like? Do you have a nice couch?"

"Oh, not the bedroom, Estella. Could you go to the office instead?" Rodrigo asked politely.

"Why?" I figured the couch in his bedroom would be more comfortable.

"The very idea of you being in another man's bedroom makes my blood boil."

Wow. He never drops the act, does he? I barely managed to hold back an exasperated laugh and simply nodded.

"We'll go to the office then, Rodrigo."

He gave me a faint smile. I could sense Anneheine was affected by it. That was proof enough that the thread of destiny was sturdier and more durable than even the specialty thread the Kartinas traded.

In Blanche's office, I bound him to a chair. Then I asked Anneheine for a change of clothes, hoping to strip from my bloodstained ones. Anneheine was polite and friendly even though we had refused her plea. It seemed she was set to be kind no matter what. She returned with an extremely frilly, expensive-looking dress. It wasn't something I wanted to wear when I had blood splattered all over me.

"Do you have anything simpler?"

"Only nightdresses."

"I'd rather wear one of those."

Anneheine looked conflicted.

"If you're concerned about my honor, don't worry. I gave up on that when I ripped my skirt and swung a sword around."

I seemed to have been right because she lowered her head for a moment before returning to her room. I didn't exchange a single word with Blanche while I waited. He seemed busy trying to devise an escape plan, but that wouldn't happen with him tied up.

"Thank you. Don't untie your father," I said, even though I had tied the knots so tightly that she wouldn't be able to do so anyway.

I entered the small bathroom attached to the office and closed the door. I removed my torn, bloodied clothes and washed off the gore staining my face and neck. Once I was clean enough, I pulled on the blue nightdress—which was unlike the simple nightdresses I wore to bed.

"It's practically a normal dress."

There was so much fabric that the skirt was as voluminous as a ballgown. The waist was cinched, and the shoulders were too poofy.

"How do you even sleep in this?"

I clicked my tongue and exited the bathroom.

Peering at Blancge and Annehein, I asked, "Did you two

have a nice chat between father and daughter while I was gone?"

Neither responded.

"You don't mind if I talk now, right?"

I was going to anyway, even if they didn't want me to. I intended to interrogate Blanche while Rodrigo interrogated Vandula. I had never intended to rest on the couch. I dragged over a chair and sat in front of Blanche.

"Who is backing you?" I asked immediately.

Blanche's gaze trembled.

CHAPTER
FORTY-SEVEN

"Oh my."

Nathaniel pricked his finger on a thorn as he fiddled with a rose.

"Your Holiness! Are you all right?"

The long queue of priests next to him took out white silk handkerchiefs and held them out to him. Nathaniel smiled faintly as he took one and compressed his finger.

"Your Holiness, you need healing magic."

"No, no. It's just a small prick from a thorn. You're overreacting." Nathaniel waved them away, and the priests left the room.

Only one person stayed behind with him.

"Julianne, I'm hurt," Nathaniel whined as he stepped before the woman, whose eyes were covered.

She parted her lips. Nathaniel placed his wounded finger in her mouth.

"Julianne, you really are... ha... so kind." His cheeks flushed. He exhaled a shaky breath.

Julianne sucked the blood from Nathaniel's finger for a

long moment, then pushed it out of her mouth with her tongue.

"Julianne?" Nathaniel called her name.

Her blindfolded face turned toward him.

"...One of the sorcerers is dead, Your Holiness."

"Oh..."

The words that finally escaped her lips after a long moment of silence were enough to ruin Nathaniel's good mood completely.

"And another will die soon."

"Can you see it?"

Julianne nodded.

"What else do you see?" Nathaniel asked in a sweet voice that didn't suit his cold expression. He caressed Julianne's cheek.

"A black and a blue dragon."

Erhart and Kartina.

"Oh my. Perhaps I should have gone to the battlefield then."

Nathaniel had changed his plan to appear on the battlefield when Estella came to see him. It would have been too risky to make a move when she was aware of his plan.

Nathaniel stroked Julianne's slender chin as he said, "I think it is time to change tactics."

The corner of Nathaniel's lips rose into a smirk. His expression, this real one that marred his features with his true intentions, differed greatly from his image as the empire's most benevolent pope.

Rodrigo's interrogation lasted until the early hours of the morning. I had fallen asleep while waiting for him after failing to obtain much more information from Blanche.

"Wake up, Estella."

I slid my eyes open at the sensation of a finger poking my cheek. "Are you done?"

Rodrigo nodded at my mumbled question.

"Did you find out anything?"

My entire body protested as I sat up from where I had been slumped over the desk. I stretched languidly.

Rodrigo shook his head. "He died."

"What? You killed him?"

Rodrigo's brows furrowed at my question. He rubbed a hand across his face. He repeated himself, clearly enunciating each word and looking extremely tired.

"No. He died."

"You should have put cloth in his mouth."

"He had to be able to speak... Oh, he didn't bite his own tongue."

"How did he die then?"

"Would you believe me if I told you he suddenly aged?"

I demanded more details, and Rodrigo glanced at Blanche sleeping on the floor before leading me over to the couch. We sat down next to each other.

"You can lie down while you listen if you are tired." Rodrigo patted his lap.

"I'm fine. You look more tired than I do," I retorted immediately, feeling like he was underestimating my physical strength.

"Pardon me then."

Only then did I realize he was really just being polite because he suddenly flopped down, putting his head on my lap.

"Rodrigo!"

He flexed his muscles as if afraid I would push him off.

"I won't push you away, so relax. You're pushing down on me."

He relaxed, and the weight on my lap became much lighter.

Rodrigo explained, "He was quite cooperative. Though he only talked about himself instead of what I wanted to hear."

Rodrigo told me about what he had talked about with Vandula. There were many more mad sorcerers here besides him. All he had found out was that there were many others in Veloki and that someone was sponsoring them with a large sum of money.

"I said I could pay more."

"And?"

"He seemed happy."

"And then?"

"He died."

"Just like that?"

Rodrigo closed his eyes and covered his face with his arm.

"Wrinkles suddenly began to appear on his face, and his black hair turned white. Liver spots appeared on his skin, which started to dry up before he collapsed to the side, completely scrawny."

"Was he in pain?"

"Not at all."

So it's not a curse or dark magic.

"I suspect that it was due to time catching up to him all at once."

"What?"

Rodrigo stood up.

"It has been twenty-five years since the mad sorcerers first made their appearance. Since they were fairly distinguished in their craft, they must have been rather old even then."

This was according to the Erhart family records.

"But how old did the sorcerers we met look?"

"Pretty young. In their thirties, at most."

"I believe they may have discovered how to use magic to stay young."

"At what cost?"

"I am sure they could not stop aging altogether. Perhaps the time they held at bay comes rushing back if they run out of mana."

Rodrigo's theory made sense.

"What I am worried about is—" Rodrigo smiled bitterly. "That those who wish for eternal youth are never good people."

I nodded.

"I feel we have gotten ourselves another mission," he observed.

"It's like getting more homework while doing homework, right?"

Rodrigo laughed, apparently amused by my comparison.

"Get some rest," he said. "We have time."

"We must go see King Franz." I shook my head.

"They are already keeping tabs on his every move. Both Blanche and Vandula knew about our meeting with His Majesty."

Our plan had failed.

"There must be another way." Rodrigo clenched his fists, evidently refusing to give up.

Right, this is the kind of man he is. He was the type of person who became more determined as the situation became more difficult.

"Hm, if we must meet with him, we should call him out here."

I decided to put my trust in him and help. I had to get into his good graces anyway, so helping Rodrigo was a given.

"How?" he asked.

I nodded over at Blanche. "His Majesty's greatest opposition is in our clutches."

I smiled as I rummaged through Blanche's desk drawers, grabbing some paper. I wrote a letter and took out Blanche's seal to close it. Then I gave the letter to Anneheine. She looked at us blearily, having just been woken up and summoned here.

"Miss Anneheine, could you help us?"

She took the letter without any complaints. It passed the palace walls early that morning, and by noon, the king's carriage arrived at the Blanche Manor.

We untied Blanche. Having lost many knights and two sorcerers, Blanche seemed to have lost his will to fight.

"I cannot cooperate."

I could understand why seeing that someone was backing him and the mad sorcerers. Rodrigo silently kicked his shins, and Blanche staggered.

"Do not make me regret letting you live."

A deep chill traced down my spine even though Rodrigo's cold words weren't directed at me.

Thinking that his calm fury was scarier, I tugged at his hand, saying, "His Majesty is waiting."

We had Blanche walking ahead of us as we headed to the reception room, where Franz was waiting.

"Sir Blanche, you may be a high-ranking and admirable minister, but how dare you make me, the king... Sir Rodrigo!"

Franz seemed extremely irritated by the fact that Blanche had summoned him via letter, as he loosed a waterfall of words until he noticed Rodrigo and me. He pushed aside the tired-looking Blanche and embraced Rodrigo.

"I was getting worried because there was no word from you after you left."

As I watched Franz's face light up and heard the concern in his voice, I wondered whether Rodrigo was popular with men as well. Then again, he was loved by everyone except the imperial family and the Kartinas. Most people were too afraid of the imperial family and the Kartinas to assist him, but I remembered that everyone was rooting for Rodrigo.

I curtsied to Franz and sat down on the couch. *You two can go on with your touching reunion.*

Blanche shuffled over to stand at the king's side.

"Please have a seat, Your Majesty."

"Yes, let's do that, Sir Rodrigo."

I had expected their passionate reunion to continue, but Rodrigo ended it. Blanche called for a butler to bring them tea.

"And leave out the poison," I added, smiling brightly at the butler as he turned away.

His back flinched visibly. The household staff at the Blanche Manor were scared senselessly. The rumor was that an intruder had taken over the manor.

I suppose that from their perspective, Rodrigo is an intruder. Blanche started it, though.

The butler soon returned with tea. I took out a silver needle I kept on me at all times and stirred the tea before offering it to Franz and Rodrigo. Franz's eyes narrowed.

"What kind of person is your lover, Sir Rodrigo?" he whispered in Rodrigo's ear.

"I am Estella Kartina." *That's enough of an explanation, right?*

Watching Franz's expression harden, I casually took a sip of tea.

"I don't need to check your teacup, do I, Sir Blanche?"

There was no way they would poison their own master.

Blanche's lips contorted before he raised his teacup.

"Kartina? You mean the family that keeps interfering with

your business affairs? Your... nemesis?"

I can hear you, you know. I wonder if he's so tactless because he was born a prince.

I turned away, doing my best to pretend I couldn't hear him.

"Your Majesty, this is not the best time to be asking about my lover. The kingdom has been swept up in a conspiracy. And it affects me negatively too," Rodrigo said.

Only then did Franz lean back and put his hands together over his stomach.

Rodrigo continued, "We were confused about the mad sorcerers joining the battle on Veloki's side. Everybody thought they had disappeared long ago. Besides, it is forbidden all across the continent to harbor the mad sorcerers. Judging by your character, Your Majesty, I believed you would never have anything to do with them."

"Of course." Franz seemed touched that Rodrigo had trusted him and smiled.

Rodrigo paused for a moment before continuing. "That is why I suspected there was something wrong in Veloki and came to see you."

"You must have been shocked to find me imprisoned."

"You were not imprisoned, Your Majesty!" Blanche piped in.

Franz glared at him coldly, and Blanche met the gaze

intently for a long time… before finally turning away.

Wow, that would have gotten him killed in the empire. Daring to glare back at the emperor when he is reprimanding you? You're practically asking to be executed. I wonder if Franz is just too easy on his subjects. But didn't he kill all of his older brothers to ascend the throne?

"Yes, you are right. You were imprisoned, and we suspected a noble named Blanche, so we needed to look into it. But then he contacted us first. In a very rude manner, I might add."

I recalled getting kidnapped. I didn't realize I was clenching my hand so tightly until the teaspoon I had been holding to stir sugar into my tea folded in half.

"Oh! I'll reimburse you for the teaspoon later." I put down the bent teaspoon and picked up Rodrigo's. "May I?"

"Of course," Rodrigo replied kindly.

Franz and Blanche stared at us exasperatedly for a while.

"Two mad sorcerers died, and we're left with Sir Blanche."

"So, you're saying I just have to kill him?" Franz straightened up.

He looked as though he was ready to kill Blanche on the spot.

Rodrigo shook his head. "Estella and I have a different plan, Your Majesty. Put Sir Blanche on the throne."

Blanche sprang to his feet, his fists clenched tightly.

"What nonsense!" he exclaimed.

Franz gestured for him to sit back down.

"Your Majesty, these two are being disrespectful..."

I burst out laughing at the sight of Blanche throwing a fit when he had been extremely disrespectful. I turned my head to the left to look at him.

"Be thankful. And you won't be on the throne for long, so enjoy it while it lasts."

CHAPTER
FORTY-EIGHT

Blanche grew so pale that he went blue, but I paid no mind to Blanche's dropped jaw. I simply ignored him and explained the plan that Rodrigo and I had discussed.

"If things don't change, all the blame will fall on you. Since Blanche committed the crime, we believe he should be the one held responsible. And for that to happen, he must be in a position to take responsibility." I turned to the king. "Your Majesty, you should say that you will take responsibility for the war dragging on for so long and step down."

"Will the kingdom's citizens stand for it?" Franz's doubts were reasonable but incorrect.

"They are surprisingly uninterested in the goings-on of the palace."

It wasn't as though anything would change for them if someone else became king. They didn't care whether Franz or Blanche was king as long as the one on the throne wasn't a tyrant.

"The nobles will be against it," Blanche said.

"Do you really think so?" I responded, smiling.

Blanche closed his mouth. How he pretended to be on Franz's side was pathetic, even after luring all the nobles away from him.

"If you abdicate, you will not be able to ascend the throne again, Your Majesty."

"Don't worry about that. The emperor won't just stand by."

Rodrigo smiled awkwardly at my comment. *Does that mean he doesn't agree with me?*

Still, I believed I was right. The emperor would not turn a blind eye to a noble ascending the throne. If someone outside of the royal bloodline took the throne, then theoretically, anyone could become king, and people would start to dream.

"And we will give the emperor a reason to intervene." Rodrigo put the final nail in the coffin.

You're as good as dead, Blanche.

"What makes you think I would cooperate with this plan?" Blanche cried out. "If I am going to die regardless, I choose to die honorably right here, right now!"

Honorably? What does this pervert know about honor?

Rodrigo plucked my teacup out of my hand.

"You can't break the teacup, Estella. You will hurt your hand."

Even in this situation, he was worried about me. I was unable to react properly because I was unsure whether I should be touched by his consistent behavior.

"What if I die?" Anneheine emerged from the small adjoining bathroom.

Wow, she was hiding in there? I looked at her with wide eyes. She had probably hidden because she was curious about our conversation. However, to me, this felt like the work of her and Rodrigo's destined connection. It was like they were inseparable.

"Anneheine!" Blanche's voice grew high-pitched.

He could be a soprano. I was ready to watch the ensuing heated discussion between father and daughter.

"You've committed a crime, so take your punishment!" she shouted. "Take responsibility for your actions! If you don't, I will kill myself."

I knew full well just how much Blanche treasured his daughter as she was his only biological child, which he thought he could never have, and figured that he would agree to our plan.

"I'm doing this for you, Anneheine... It is difficult for a young woman to survive on her own in the world. All I wanted was to leave you with a fortune and enough authority so that no one would dare to oppose you." An unending train of Blanche's heartbreaking excuses followed.

Rodrigo fidgeted in his seat, looking uncomfortable, and Franz smiled exasperatedly.

And me? I just continued to drink my tea. *The tea is quite exquisite. How befitting of the highest-ranking noble in the kingdom.* That was all that was on my mind.

"All for me, you say? I don't want any of that! I want to live a conscientious life even if I have to be poor!"

She was very naive. No, she was as righteous, kind, and pure as a heroine ought to be. However, to me, living my second life and having been thrust into a novel for my second life at that, it all sounded naive. *Does she even know what it's like to be poor?*

"That's enough. I can't listen to any more of this," Franz interrupted the two.

"Oh my, Your Majesty, please forgive my insolence." Anneheine, who had been yelling so much that her cheeks were visibly red, hurriedly wiped away her tears and formally greeted the king.

"It's all right. I am glad to see that you are very different from your father."

See? I knew she was the heroine. If any other young noblewoman had caused such a scene in front of a royal, she would have been executed on the spot.

"Are you tired?"

As my mind grew twisted yet again, Rodrigo spoke up. He was looking at me—not Annehine.

"Have you been staring at me this whole time?" I responded curtly, feeling like my pettiness had been caught, but Rodrigo just smiled and nodded.

"Did it take you this long to realize?"

He never drops the act. I pushed him away as he tried to lean in closer and turned to look at Franz, Blanche, and Anneheine again.

"I deserve to die, Your Majesty. My father's disloyalty cannot be paid for with his life alone, so I deserve to die with him." Anneheine lowered herself to her knees.

"No, Your Majesty! My daughter has nothing to do with any of this!"

How touching. I'm already sick of all this drama. I rose from my seat and stood in front of Franz.

I asked, "May I interfere a bit with the Veloki Kingdom matters?"

I had already done so quite a bit. *How shameless of me to ask.* "Go ahead."

Perhaps it was because I was Rodrigo's lover, but Franz treated me politely.

"We will take Miss Anneheine hostage to ensure Sir Blanche's cooperation. Until all of this is over, I mean."

"You nasty—" Blanche could not finish his insult as Rodrigo kicked him in the back.

"Did I not tell you to be polite to Estella?"

Whether it was because Rodrigo had failed to pull his punches or because too many shocking things had happened, Blanche fainted. Ultimately, our plan was approved without the consent—though it was strange to ask a criminal for consent in the first place—of the person involved.

"Your Majesty, you should take your forces with you and stay at your summer house in the capital."

"You need not worry about me, Sir Rodrigo."

"We... will win the war."

"All right."

Rodrigo planned to kill the minister in charge of the kingdom's defense while he was in Veloki.

"I will command all troops to withdraw. That will be my last order as king." Franz seemed bitter.

"You are only taking a short break. Please stay alive."

The new king's supporting factions were bound to try and dispose of the abdicated king. Franz would almost certainly have to deal with a swarm of assassins. He was taking a huge risk by cooperating with our plan.

Among everyone here, the person least negatively impacted was probably Anneheine.

She looked flushed, evidently happy at the thought of leaving Blanche's side and coming with us. I watched

Anneheine's girlish enthusiasm before turning away.

The sun was setting.

"It's time to leave."

Rodrigo nodded at my words.

"I am back."

Rodrigo entered the carriage that Anneheine and I were sitting in. He was holding a box. It was large enough to fit a person's head.

"His Majesty called him here, so it was easy to kill him."

So the defense minister's head is in there. I mourned the man who must not have seen his death coming and scooted to the side so Rodrigo could sit beside me. However, Anneheine moved to sit next to me, and both Rodrigo and I looked at her in surprise.

"The carriage is small, so I thought you should sit alone since you have a box with you as well." Anneheine was unnecessarily considerate.

"Anneheine is right."

I felt silly for expecting him to sit next to me. Rodrigo raised his eyebrows, apparently displeased, but finally sighed and sat down. The carriage began to move.

"Estella!"

As soon as I exited the carriage, Ayla embraced me. Ada copied her. Devlon ran up to us and took the box that Rodrigo was holding.

"The Velokian army has raised a white flag."

"I know."

"What happened?"

"I'll explain later. Get packed up. We're returning to the capital."

At Rodrigo's order, Devlon began to busy himself with preparations. I couldn't move a muscle, squashed between Ada and Ayla. My sisters repeatedly stroked my face.

"Did something happen?" they demanded affectionately. "Did you eat properly? You look like you lost weight. You're beautiful regardless, but still. Let's feed you some meat first, Estella."

Ayla and Ada began to nag Porter.

"You want me to go and buy some meat right now?"

"You idiot! I'm telling you to go and find the best restaurant in the area."

Porter had to use one of his precious sheets of magic paper just to find a restaurant because Ayla and Ada were so insistent.

"By the way, who's that girl?" Ada and Ayla pointed at Anneheine, who was standing awkwardly behind me.

CHAPTER
FORTY-NINE

"That bastard Rodrigo! Is this his secret lover?"

We had arrived in the evening, so we couldn't head straight to the capital. We decided to stay behind instead of using a portal nearby because there were still things to clear with Rodrigo. However, Ada and Ayla were already jumping to conclusions.

"No, I swear! I only met him for the first time yesterday!"

Anneheine waved her hands in denial, but my sisters ignored her words and kept glaring at her. With a sigh, I nibbled the warm bread Porter had managed to get us. It had been a while since I had eaten such warm and soft bread. I breathed in the scent.

I was used to Ayla and Ada's fussing and misunderstanding. Anneheine would be slightly inconvenienced, but I knew that butting in wouldn't help her, either. *I feel like things will only get worse if I chime in.*

"Who do you think you are, sitting there all shamelessly and eating our bread!" Ada snapped with more outrage than the question warranted.

Anneheine froze. Looking at her, I concluded that I couldn't just sit back and watch any longer. *This is the female lead, Ada. Technically, I'm the shameless one who got in her way.* I put down my bread and took Anneheine's hand. She blinked at me, eyes wide like a doe's.

"I will take you somewhere safer."

Erharts over the Kartinas. That was where she belonged, after all.

"Estella! You don't need to be nice to her!" Ayla jumped up from her seat, incensed.

I turned back to her. "Ayla, Ada, judging by how furious you are, I guess you acknowledge Rodrigo as my lover now."

Their mouths snapped shut. It was easy to see that Ada and Ayla had accepted my relationship with Rodrigo just based on the way they treated him. They were simply refusing to acknowledge it due to their pride and because they loved me so dearly.

As expected, even though they had insulted Anneheine for being Rodrigo's supposed side piece, my comment about them acknowledging Rodrigo shut them up.

"I'll be back. I'll finish my meal when I'm back." I added the last part before they could start nagging and hold me back for not eating my dinner.

"Let's go, come on." I pulled Anneheine by the hand.

She followed me without objection. My tent wasn't far from Rodrigo's, and his tent was easy to find. The space in front of his tent was noticeably wide. As we passed, I caught sight of familiar faces. It was Gunther and Devlon. One of Gunther's legs was missing.

I had no trouble figuring out that the Kartina thread was to blame. My heart sank, but I didn't let it show.

"Hi," I managed, searching for something better to say. "I like your..." The only thing I could offer in a subdued voice was a compliment. "I like your crutches."

Gunther seemed pleased—his frown melted away.

He said, "Thank you. Are you here to see His Grace?"

"Is he inside?"

"He is in a meeting with his advisors, but I will let him know you are here."

I was already being treated as the archduchess. I held on to Anneheine more tightly. The thought that I had usurped the role that was rightfully hers tormented me. Everything's timing had been terrible.

It would have been better for her to appear once I had taken care of everything, and it was hard to let go of Rodrigo at the moment. The Kartinas would never stand for it if Rodrigo got together with Anneheine right now.

So complicated. I shook my head.

Devlon emerged from the tent again.

"He says you should come in right away."

As soon as he finished his sentence, people began to leave Rodrigo's tent in waves. They bowed their heads once they caught sight of Anneheine and me.

"He is such a caring lover," Anneheine whispered to me, sounding envious.

He's supposed to be your lover, actually. I held back the urge to tell her this as we entered the tent. The table where the advisors had sat was in disarray. Maps, flag pins, and wooden dolls had been strewn across it.

Rodrigo was clearing the table. Normally, the advisors would have cleaned up after themselves. However, it seemed he had been left to do the cleanup himself because he sent them all away as soon as I came by.

"Just leave it."

"It won't take long. It would be better for the table to be cleared if we want to have tea." Rodrigo glanced at Anneheine and spoke informally.

Even that appeared to me like a decision made because of her, and I was reminded of the red string of fate. *An unbreakable connection, they say.*

"What brings you here this late, Estella?" he asked me.

The table was clear. He put a kettle over a small brazier

and began to boil some water. As Anneheine and I sat down, he brought us two clean cups and served us tea. Anneheine's eyes sparkled.

"Tea made by Sir Rodrigo! What an honor!" Anneheine was very sociable.

Rodrigo seemed bashful at her compliment and raised the kettle.

"I learned it for the woman I love." He sent a gentle look my way, but I avoided his gaze.

Anneheine blushed at his words. I felt like a third wheel.

"I thought you only had alcohol," I said.

"I had tea brought here for my lover, who kept fearlessly showing up."

The word "lover" made my heart flutter. Rodrigo kept trying to meet my eyes, so I turned my head away completely.

"Please take good care of Miss Anneheine," I said. I wanted to get out of his tent as soon as possible. "I can't have her stay in my tent."

"So you want her to stay in mine?" Rodrigo's tone was sharp.

The air around us suddenly grew cold. Anneheine glanced between us, watching warily.

"My sisters are harassing her."

"She's a hostage, Estella. It's fine if she gets harassed a little."

Has he always wanted to be so informal with me? His words

sounded far too natural.

I said, "This is all for your friend."

"If you insist, Estella, I can have another tent prepared for her," Rodrigo said with a finality that made it seem like he didn't intend to continue this discussion.

"Rodrigo! She's a woman. And a beautiful one at that. I trust you to be a gentleman, but I don't trust all of your men."

"Estella!" He was angry.

"Am I wrong?"

Rodrigo pressed his lips together. He knew too well what stress and exhausted soldiers were capable of. It was probably why he insisted on her staying in my tent despite knowing I wouldn't be comfortable with it.

"I didn't think that it would make you uncomfortable, Estella. I'm sorry. But I'm offended by your idea of having her stay in my tent."

This was the first time he had become angry with me. I had, of course, done my best not to anger him, but even when he had reason to, he never got angry with me. When the Kartinas destroyed his greenhouse, for example. He should have gotten angry with me then, not now.

"Rodrigo."

"I apologize for interrupting, but..." Anneheine started.

Rodrigo and I turned to look at her simultaneously. She

flinched like a rabbit facing a predator and continued, her hands clutched together tightly.

"My opinion probably doesn't matter, but I prefer to stay with Lady Estella."

Hey! My jaw dropped in exasperation. *What's with her? She should be spending time with Rodrigo as much as possible to get closer to him.*

"Listen to her, Estella," Rodrigo said, crossing his arms over his chest triumphantly.

Ugh.

"If you're uncomfortable, I will have my men move you to a bigger tent."

"It's fine."

I had no intention of aggravating the soldiers. They already had to deal with the long march to the capital, starting tomorrow.

"Why don't you return to your tent? You don't seem well enough to have tea."

You're just as annoyed as I am. I glared at Rodrigo for making all this my fault. Then I turned on my heel. I could sense Anneheine following me after watching us warily. I walked silently. The soldiers who recognized me bowed their heads. I raised my hand to greet them and returned to my tent. Ayla and Ada were still there.

"Where were you, Estella?"

"Weren't you going to get rid of her?"

I didn't have the energy to reply. As soon as I sat down, Jane arrived with a bowl of soup she had reheated for me.

"I can't even lift a spoon." I was just mumbling to myself, but as soon as my sisters heard me, they sat down next to me and began to spoon-feed me.

I felt slightly embarrassed as Anneheine's eyes widened, but I couldn't keep paying attention to her reactions. I decided to stop caring about her.

"He won?"

Detheus had just received the report on the war's outcome against the Veloki Kingdom. It was great news to hear first thing in the morning. However, he did not seem very happy. The attendant bowed his head.

"When is Rodrigo returning?"

"Most likely in one week."

"I suppose His Majesty will hold an extravagant banquet to celebrate his return."

The attendant did not answer and simply lowered his head. He could tell that his master was unhappy.

"He deserves it. I am glad to hear of our victory."

There was no praise for the general who had led the troops to victory.

A long silence followed.

"I should meet with Kalen." Detheus, who had pressed his lips together, finally spoke up again as he got to his feet.

The attendant turned on his heel and hurried to send a message to the Kartina Manor. That afternoon, Kalen went to see Crown Prince Detheus.

"You have summoned me, Your Highness?"

Normally, Kalen would not have come. He always avoided Detheus's calls with all kinds of excuses. However, now that he was standing in for Count Kartina, he couldn't simply ignore a summons from the palace. Kalen had to dress in formal attire and come to meet Detheus.

"Sit. It hurts my neck to look up at you."

Kalen sat. Soon, the attendants served steaming tea and chilled dessert, but neither Kalen nor Detheus touched any food. They sat, for a long time, in silence.

Finally, just as the silence became unbearable, Detheus spoke up. "I hear Rodrigo was victorious."

"The victory belongs to the empire, not Sir Rodrigo," Kalen clarified.

It was true that Rodrigo had much to do with the victory, but Kalen didn't want him to become a war hero. He still didn't approve of Rodrigo as Estella's lover. To Kalen, Rodrigo was nothing but a thief who had stolen away his lovely and adorable baby sister.

"It gladdens me to hear you say so. Rodrigo is a great knight, but he doesn't seem to be a very good man. What do you think?"

"I agree, Your Highness."

"Someone like him needs a woman from a strong family."

Kalen raised his eyebrows.

"Like us, the Philemon family." Detheus smiled.

Kalen could tell what Detheus was up to just by looking at his smile.

"What a great idea, Your Highness."

"I knew you were clever. That's why I like you."

"I do not swing that way," Kalen responded with a joke.

Detheus laughed. "Me either."

Kalen ran into Hela on his way out of the imperial palace. "Mother?"

He hadn't heard that they would return to the capital, and mother and son stood there, surprised at seeing each other at the imperial palace instead of home.

"What brings you here?" Hela asked her son, whom she hadn't seen in ages, instead of inquiring about his well-being.

"Crown Prince Detheus summoned me here."

"I suppose those foxes think alike."

Kalen sensed that the emperor must have called Hela after hearing those words.

"Are you on your way to meet him?"

"I am. Our carriage is outside, so wait there. I won't be long."

Hela walked past Kalen and into the imperial palace. The emperor must have called for her because the war had been won—she was curious to see his reaction.

CHAPTER
FIFTY

Hela returned in no time from her meeting with the emperor.

"What did he say?"

Neither mother nor son was particularly interested in a touching reunion. Kalen said simply, "We discussed Sir Rodrigo's reward."

"What will he give him?" Hela asked.

"The crown princess."

"The apple doesn't fall far from the tree," she commented. "Did the crown prince say the same thing?"

"He did."

Hela pressed her lips together at Kalen's reply.

Kalen was curious about what Hela was thinking. He knew she wasn't fond of Rodrigo either, so he had expected her to rejoice at the news. However, that didn't seem to be the case.

"Does it bother you, Mother?" Kalen asked carefully.

"Why would I be bothered?" Hela responded casually, but Kalen could tell right away. *She's angry.*

Ada, Ayla, and I decided to return via a portal. As I was gathering my things to head to the portal, Anneheine twiddled her thumbs and looked at me. Her puppy-dog eyes were distracting.

"There are only so many people who can use the portal at once. Though it would be nice if you could come along."

There was no helping it. It wasn't as though I could leave Jane behind. Nor did I want to.

"What about me?"

"Sir Rodrigo will take good care of you," I said to her and looked at him. We hadn't talked since our fight in his tent last night.

Rodrigo shrugged and shook his head. He signaled that he wouldn't be taking care of her, but I knew. He was far too kindhearted to ignore Anneheine if she had no one to turn to. He might not take great care of her, but she at least wouldn't starve or need to deal with unwanted attention from the soldiers.

"Stay safe, Anneheine," I said. "And you too, Rodrigo."

Rodrigo simply nodded.

He's so petty. I quickly left the tent. Thinking about the two of them alone ruined my mood.

"This way, My Lady." Jane, holding our horses' reins, waved over to me. Although he had talked about how valuable war horses were, Rodrigo had loaned us five. One each for me, Jane, Ayla, Ada, and Porter.

The war camp was mostly cleared. They could start their march to the capital by noon at the latest.

As I leaped onto the saddle, Rodrigo handed me the reins and bid me farewell. "See you at the capital."

I was certain that he, too, didn't want to leave things awkward between us, but neither of us apologized. I wasn't sure why I should apologize. It seemed as though Rodrigo felt the same way.

"Let's go, Estella."

I took the reins from Rodrigo. I could tell by his eyes that he had much to say, but we didn't have any more time to talk. Ada spurred on her horse and went ahead. We urged the horses forward one after another, keeping a single file line as we left the war camp.

Hela was there to greet me once we arrived at the capital.

"Mother!" I ran into her arms once I exited the portal, calling her with childlike excitement. I really was glad to see her, but I also didn't want her to scold me.

Hela rubbed my back and kissed my forehead, whispering that she loved me. "Are you hurt anywhere, my darling?"

Instead of scolding me for running off to the battlefield again, Hela was busy worrying about me.

"Ada, Ayla, and Jane. Come see me." However, my sisters and Jane could not avoid her nagging. Hela sent me upstairs to rest, leaving behind Ada, Ayla, and Jane.

As I left them, I pressed my hands together apologetically and mimed an apology toward them behind Hela's back. Ada and Ayla grinned widely and gestured for me to go upstairs, but Jane did not.

"I hate you," she mouthed.

I'm so sorry, Jane. I hurried away, thinking about pretty dresses and jewelry to buy for her.

I bathed with my maids' help and fell asleep in my soft bed. It had been a while since I could sleep without a care in the world, and when I awoke, it was late at night. Stretching my arms up high, I noticed a tray with snacks on my table. Next to it was a small note. As I unfolded it, I caught sight of cute, rounded handwriting. It was from Jane.

It read, "Eat this when you get up, My Lady. My loyalty to you isn't strong enough to wake you right now."

Hela must have been harsh with her because I could tell how mad Jane was. I smiled at her cute complaint and sat down to eat. It was sandwiches and a sweet drink. Jane probably didn't wake me up because I was so sound asleep. I had no doubt whatsoever about her loyalty.

Picking up the tray, I moved to sit at the table beside the window. I pulled it open to look out at the night sky. There was no moon tonight. Rodrigo had said they intended to ride through the night to reach the capital, but it seemed too dark for that.

It would take him at least ten days to arrive at the capital. Counting the days somehow made my heart feel empty.

"I must be hungry." I took a big bite of my sandwich.

"Do you have any extra?"

I turned around with the sandwich still in my mouth. A slender man was leaning against my door. Before I could reply, he started toward me. I couldn't see his face clearly, but his gait and slim silhouette were familiar.

"Using magic takes a lot of energy. I'm hungry, so if you're not going to eat that, I will." Rodrigo reached out his hand and snatched the sandwich from my mouth.

"...Rodrigo?" I stared at him in disbelief.

"Yes, it's me, your lover," he said before taking a big bite out of my sandwich.

He makes it look delicious.

"What are you doing here?"

"I couldn't sleep because my lover left me with a strange woman."

"What?"

"Did you really want me to share a room with Anneheine?" he asked after putting down the rest of the sandwich and downing my drink.

"You make it sound strange. I was only asking you to take care of her."

"You dragged her all the way to my tent. Is that all you have to say?" Rodrigo clicked his tongue.

I pressed my lips together and let silence fill the room. I turned my head to stare at nothing, feigning looking out the window, and Rodrigo watched me. His gaze on my cheek was practically painful.

"Do you hate me now?"

I felt dazed momentarily when Rodrigo finally opened his mouth. "What did you say?"

"I asked if you don't like me anymore."

"What do you mean?"

"You keep pushing Anneheine on me."

"Pushing?"

Rodrigo nodded. I crossed my arms and looked at him. He seemed to have noticed my annoyed expression because he straightened up.

"Don't forget that she's your hostage."

"Our hostage, to be exact."

I wondered if he had always been such a meticulous and argumentative man. Suddenly tired, I let out a long sigh. Rodrigo sighed along with me. And then we both became silent again. Facing each other, we tried to speak up... but failed. Frustrating.

It seemed as though there was no clear path forward. No matter what we tried, our conversations kept going in circles. To settle this matter, I had to tell Rodrigo that Anneheine was meant to be his lover.

But will he believe me?

He would probably say I was saying strange things because I was tired. I refused to talk any further.

"Do we really need to fight because of Lady Anneheine?" His words hit me like a hammer. "I want to talk about you and me, not Lady Anneheine."

"But she's in the middle of all this," I said quietly.

"Is she? Or are you trying to push her between us, Estella?"

Oh. I was at a loss for words. Rodrigo was right. Rodrigo had absolutely no interest in Anneheine. Though I didn't know how Anneheine felt, she wasn't making any moves to get close to Rodrigo either. I was the one who kept pushing them together.

"You should stop unless your intention is to break up with me."

Wouldn't it be annulling our agreement, not breaking up?

"Do you wish to break up?"

"Not yet."

Rodrigo's eyes turned dark, seemingly displeased.

"Or do you like love triangles?"

"No," I said. Even the thought of a love triangle made me gag. I intended to leave before that ever happened.

"Fine then. We agree that we will not break up and continue to be loyal to each other."

I wanted to object to his conclusion, but somehow, I felt too tired. Our verbal sparring had worn me out. I nodded slowly. For a moment, we simply stared at each other. Neither Rodrigo nor I knew how much time had passed.

"Are you falling asleep?" he asked after a moment.

Am I?

I didn't think I was, but when Rodrigo said so, I felt like I was falling asleep. My eyelids grew heavy. My view of Rodrigo grew smaller and smaller as my eyelids drooped.

"From now on, you have agreed to lend me..." Rodrigo said something, but I couldn't quite remember what he said. "Your answer."

I wanted to lie down on my bed, so I just nodded. I heard

him laugh, apparently satisfied. Then my body was suddenly lifted into the air. I could hear Rodrigo's even heartbeat. He laid me down on my bed and placed a pillow beside me.

What a player.

In the short time we had spent together, he discovered my sleeping habits. Though I was annoyed, my lips kept curving into a smile. I felt like I would have a delightful dream tonight.

The next day went by in a flash. The Kartinas had returned to their usual routine, and we hardly saw each other. Ayla and Ada went off to the western border to assist Stefan, and Hela was busy inspecting the county's affairs that Kalen had managed. Kalen was nowhere to be seen.

"What did I tell you would happen if you mixed these two chemicals, My Lady?"

I had to take remedial classes in poison-making because of the upcoming level exam.

"I don't know, Madam." I smiled brightly, looking utterly clueless and driving my teacher insane.

"You're too much, My Lady! If you cannot pass the level exam again, you will have to take lessons with your younger cousins!"

Oh, right! I do! Still, there was no helping it. If I passed this exam, I would have to go out on missions as a Kartina. And I didn't want to do that.

"There's nothing I can do about it, Madam." I slumped my shoulders, looking incredibly disappointed.

My teacher sighed over my head. "Let us end here for today." She sighed again and again before letting me leave.

My footsteps were light as I returned to my room. Only to be completely startled.

"Rodrigo!" I exclaimed. He was in my room again. "Did you just come out of my bathroom?"

CHAPTER
FIFTY-ONE

He came out of my bathroom all wet. Rodrigo was dressed in nothing but his pants. The pronounced lines of his muscles were on full display. I squeezed my eyes shut before opening them again. Rodrigo was still there. He was standing there without a shirt and drying his hair with a towel.

He tilted his head to the side and asked, "Are you not coming in?"

It was hard to go in even though it was my room.

"This is what they call trespassing," I shot at him curtly.

Rodrigo's eyebrows drooped down.

"Do you not remember? You gave me permission."

He tossed his towel on a chair and turned his back to me. His wide shoulders and the shadows cast by his taut muscles came into view. I didn't want to look, but my gaze kept drifting, and I stared as my cheeks became hot. Then, Rodrigo put on a shirt, and somehow I felt disappointed. I fanned myself to cool down my flushed face.

"What do you mean, you got my permission?" I asked him.

"I knew you wouldn't remember. I told you last night that

I will be sleeping over from now on since I cannot stay with Miss Anneheine."

Did he? I may have heard something like that right before I dozed off. Judging by Rodrigo's solemn expression, he wasn't lying. I wanted to argue, but then I noticed that Rodrigo looked unwell.

"You... used magic, didn't you?"

Rodrigo shrugged. "How could I be here without using magic?"

I pressed my lips together. Rodrigo's magic was still unstable. I was sure his body would pay a toll if he continued using it.

"Don't strain yourself."

I couldn't order him to leave immediately because it would require him to use more magic. I sighed and checked whether my bed was made before sitting on the couch.

I scolded him, "Get some rest."

Rodrigo clicked his tongue, apparently exasperated. "What are you doing?"

"Getting ready to sleep." I hugged a cushion to my chest and closed my eyes.

"Sleep in your bed, Estella."

"I can just sleep tomorrow morning, so don't worry. You're the one who has to travel on horseback."

I had simply made my decision based on what would be most efficient. Rodrigo seemed unhappy with my decision and leaned over in front of the couch instead of going to bed. As he leaned closer, I could smell my own scent on him.

"I see that you used my things without permission too," I said.

"I borrowed them. I'll repay you tenfold soon."

It wasn't that I thought it was a waste. My chest felt strangely fluttery, so I just said whatever popped into my mind. As I stayed there, not moving a muscle and keeping my eyes closed, Rodrigo leaned in closer. His hair felt cold against my forehead.

"Breathe. I'm not going to bite," he said.

I must have been holding my breath without realizing it. I peered through my eyelashes. The bridge of his perfect nose came into view. *I can't deny that I fall for good looks.*

"Fine, I will, so back off," I said, trying to shake off this fluttery feeling. "And do you think I'd even let you bite me?" *I can protect myself just fine.*

"I am aware of that." Rodrigo smiled as he straightened up.

He sat on the edge of the table and looked at me. He looked like he had much to say, so I sat up to give him my full attention.

I said, "Rodrigo, you have a long day of traveling ahead of

you tomorrow. Let's not squabble and just go to sleep."

"I would very much like to sleep too. But how am I supposed to feel comfortable enough to sleep if the owner of this room is sleeping on the couch?"

"What is it that you want?" It was laughable that he was lamenting about my discomfort when he was the intruder.

"We should sleep together."

"Not going to happen." I hugged my couch cushion tighter and shook my head.

"I will sleep on the couch then."

"That's—"

"Then, should we sleep together?" Rodrigo said, cutting me off.

A staring contest began. Rodrigo smiled cheekily, and I squeezed my cushion even tighter as my lips formed a firm line. The silence between us went on for a long time. In the end, I gave up.

"Let's sleep."

"Where?"

"On the bed."

"Together?"

I threw a cushion at him, and he caught it easily.

"Don't cross this line."

I lay down next to Rodrigo and placed a cushion between

us to mark our territories. My bed was quite large, so there was more than enough room for both of us. Rodrigo lay on his back on the other side of the cushion and closed his eyes. The lamplight cast shadows against his eyelashes that stretched out across his face.

He didn't even say goodnight. I stuck my tongue out at him.

"I can tell what you are doing."

Sheesh, does he have a third eye? "I'm not doing anything."

Once the light was off, every sound became clearer. The loudest was Rodrigo's breathing. It was even and calm, almost like a lullaby. I was amazed at how breathing could sound so melodious. As I lay there, I thought of Anneheine, who would be all alone. Anneheine was the one who belonged next to Rodrigo, and it made me feel uneasy to think about how I was taking her place.

"Is Anneheine doing well?" I asked quietly in the dark.

"Probably." He sounded entirely uninterested, as if Anneheine was an object.

"Rodrigo, you should be nice to her."

"This occurred to me before, but do you owe Miss Anneheine some debt?"

"No."

"Then why are you so good to her, like you owe her something?"

I could feel the bed underneath me jostle. He had probably rolled over and was staring down at me, his head propped up with his elbow. I could sense his gaze even through the darkness.

"I just... pity her." I came up with a random excuse.

"You should pity me more than her. Can't you be nicer to me?"

His somber voice pulled at my heartstrings. I found myself unable to reply. It was not a wish I could fulfill.

Sunlight hit my face, and I opened my eyes. Instinctively, I reached out to check the spot next to me. Rodrigo's side of the bed was empty. It was neat and tidy, as if he had never been there.

"He didn't even say goodbye."

"Pardon, My Lady?" Jane asked.

Oh! I hope she didn't see Rodrigo. I smiled at her, saying, "Never mind."

As I got out of bed, I studied Jane's expression. She was humming, which made me think that she probably didn't notice Rodrigo coming and going. Relieved, I exhaled a sigh of relief. Wondering about Rodrigo, I washed up and ate the food brought to me by an attendant.

"By the way, My Lady, I heard you would be taking lessons with your young cousins starting today."

"Oh..." I had forgotten.

I had given up on the poison and sword-fighting tests. That meant that I would be taking classes with Uncle Schubert's son Gilther, Uncle Schuron's son Billian, and his daughter Roa. Gilther was the only one my age, and Roa was ten years younger.

Adorable Roa. I smiled thinking about Roa's chubby cheeks. Unlike Gilther and Billian, who weren't cute, Roa was a lovely kid. She even had talent as a Kartina. How unfortunate.

"Right. Are we taking classes here?"

"Yes, you will be doing hands-on training at the monster hunting grounds," Jane said as if it wasn't a big deal.

However, I was worried. It was inevitable for the teachers to lose sight of everyone during hands-on training. That meant that students would often attack each other, not just the monsters. It was commonplace for Kalen, Ada, and Ayla to attack each other. The likelihood that Gilther, who was my age, would attack me was close to a hundred percent. *No, more like a thousand percent.*

"Are you worried?" Jane asked.

I smiled awkwardly and waved my hand dismissively. "Not at all."

I was honestly distraught that I might be unable to hold back my anger and end up killing Gilther.

Gilther K1artina and I had never once gotten along.

It happened at my tenth birthday party...

"You're really ugly."

That was the first thing Gilther had said to me. Kalen, Ada, and Ayla had, of course, flipped out and beaten Gilther to a pulp that day. Uncle Schubert had demanded that Stefan pay for his medical care, and Stefan had paid him more than necessary in an attempt to get him to shut up about it.

Uncle Schubert must've scolded him because Gilther has avoided me ever since that day, but he has never stopped glaring at me. Every once in a while, he'd send me threatening letters. It was obvious who they were from, but I never told anybody and just quietly burned them. I didn't need to deal with him.

However, things would be different if we were going to be taking lessons together. More importantly, I couldn't understand why Gilther hadn't advanced to a higher level yet. He wasn't particularly outstanding, but he was as good as the average Kartina.

Maybe something happened on the test day.

Something felt off. Whatever the case may be, I was planning on failing the next test that would take place in two months as well, so I would only have to see Gilther for two months.

He wouldn't fail again, right? If he did, he would have to take his name off the Kartina family registry because Schubert would be too ashamed of him. He might even run away on his own accord.

"Hello, Lady Estella!" the guards stationed outside the monster forest greeted me with gusto. Their voices were loud enough to make my ears ring.

"Great work, everyone." I smiled brightly as I complimented them a bit more before heading into the forest.

In the forest's shadows, the air immediately grew thicker. For some reason, the air in areas inhabited by monsters was thicker than the air we were used to breathing. It felt like gravity was stronger here, so it took more energy to move around. I wasn't sure if gravity really was stronger or whether this was purely psychological. Science was not at all advanced here because everything was quite irrationally explained by magic or mythology in this world.

I put my hand on my sword's hilt at my waist and wove my way toward the monster forest's center.

"Estella!"

In the middle of the forest was a small clearing meant for training. There was a wooden shack as well as a table and chairs made from rough-hewn wood. Roa was sitting on one of the chairs, her brown hair in two braids. She seemed happy to see me as she jumped on top of her chair and waved.

"Roa!"

I hadn't seen her in a long time. The Kartina cousins weren't close, so I couldn't see Roa very often. I saw her last year, no, two years ago, on her birthday. Since then, Roa had grown much taller, and her hair was longer as well. Her face looked less round, and her nose was a bit bigger. Though she still had some childlike features, she no longer had the babyface. I was a little sad but proud of her at the same time to see her grow up so nicely. I picked her up and hugged her.

"Don't touch my sister."

A low and curt voice came from behind. Billian.

"Put down your dagger first," I told him, not turning around as I kept hugging Roa.

His blade was pushing against my back. *Kids these days have such bad manners. Sure, he's a Kartina, but pulling out a dagger before even saying hello?* I didn't want to comment on bad parenting, but I had no choice.

CHAPTER
FIFTY-TWO

At least Stefan and Hela taught me to greet someone before I kill them. Of course, there were exceptions to this rule.

"I told you to put down your dagger."

Billian was only sixteen. My birthday was coming up, so he was basically two years younger than me.

"Make me."

Billian had always tried to challenge me even though he knew he couldn't win.

I sighed quietly and set Roa down on her chair.

"Hold on, Roa."

"I'll stab you if you keep moving."

You don't have the guts. I ducked and turned around. At the same time, I swept Billian's leg out from under him and pushed him over with my shoulder. There was a resounding *thud* as he hit the ground. The dagger he had been holding went flying.

I said, "Billian, you have to greet your elders when you meet them."

He looked up at me from where he landed on his behind. He didn't look upset about being beaten.

Instead, he said, "So, I hear you're hanging out with Erhart these days?"

Gossip seemed to have spread quite far, seeing that Billian, who was usually uninterested in such things, was bringing it up.

"How is that any of your business?"

"Behave yourself, Estella."

It was strange to hear him say my name.

"What?"

"I said, behave yourself, Estella."

He must've thought that I hadn't heard him well because he repeated his words. It was strange for him to advise me. It even sounded like he was worried about me.

"Are you... not feeling well or something?" My reaction was totally warranted, but Billian's face contorted into a grimace.

"Whatever, I don't care!" he shouted, making Roa grab my skirt in shock.

"Everyone is so energetic today."

Our swordsmanship teacher appeared. He was dressed in shabby clothing, and the long scar across his face, which displayed his notoriety across the continent, wasn't pleasant to look at. I preferred honorable swordsmanship. This new teacher looked as though he would be teaching very different techniques. And my assumption turned out to be correct.

"Kill your enemies using any means necessary."

After he said this, he climbed up a tall tree, saying he would assess our skills.

"Gilther isn't here yet!" Billian said.

Our teacher sat on a tree branch and dangled his feet.

"He's arrived early and has been practicing. So do not worry and go wild."

A cloud of powder descended on us. It got all over me, Roa, and Billian.

"What a nasty teacher," I mumbled, and Billian and Roa turned to look at me.

"Do you know what this is?"

"A scent that riles up male monsters."

It was a pheromone that female monsters emitted during mating season. Billian, who understood what that meant, flushed while Roa tilted her head in confusion.

"I'll explain it to you later, Roa. Hold your sword properly."

The custom-made sword for Roa was lovely and cute, but the blade was sharp.

She nodded. "I will."

A few moments later, a thunderous noise shook the earth. Not just one, but dozens of monsters came leaping into sight over our heads. Fortunately, they were low-level monsters that weren't particularly strong, even though they were big.

"Get ready, Roa!"

I fought while trying my best to protect Roa. I knew this wasn't good for her training, but it was my instinct to protect a child.

We slashed at them and kept them back for what felt like forever... but I couldn't tell how much time had passed. Only when the powder our teacher had dumped on us was washed away by the blood of all the monsters did the wave of monsters cease.

Our ragged breathing filled the air. It hadn't been a difficult fight. However, defeating so many monsters in such a short amount of time was tiring.

"What's next, sir?" I looked up.

Lessons at Kartina Manor had more to do with whether the goal was achieved than whether the allotted time had been used up. If our teacher's goal today had simply been to test our skills, we could leave. *I really hope that's the case.*

Monster blood was thicker than human blood, so it felt worse on my skin. It was hot and viscous, so the way it slowly slid down my arms and legs whenever I walked was disgusting.

"Sir?"

When we didn't hear an answer, Billian called out for our teacher. However, there was still no answer.

"Estella!" Billian suddenly leaped at me.

We got tangled up and fell over in a pile of limbs. His shoulders blocked my vision.

"What the heck are you doing?" As I was bowled over, my head hit a pillar. I held my ringing head and pushed Billian off me.

"Stop moving, idiot," Billian growled.

Past his shoulder, I could see Roa standing in front of us, holding her sword. A long shadow fell over the top of her head.

Gilther said, "Have the ugly cousins decided to band together?"

"I can't move another step," Anneheine announced.

They had stopped for a brief rest.

Rodrigo studied her. "What do you mean?"

"Can't we go a bit more slowly?" she asked.

He wondered whether she understood she was a hostage. Rodrigo was exasperated with her for not only demanding a carriage but now also asking for a change in their schedule. *If it weren't for Estella...* Rodrigo clenched his fists momentarily, imagining leaving Anneheine behind in the middle of the forest.

"We cannot."

Anneheine bit her lip at his firm refusal. "Sir Rodrigo, I'm not just asking for my own sake. Look at your men."

She gestured over to the resting soldiers. Just as she had said, they looked exhausted.

"And?" Rodrigo asked nonchalantly.

"Pardon?"

"They are tired. So what?" he said. "We have told the emperor that we would arrive at the capital within a week. Are you saying we should ignore that and take our time?"

"But if the men are tired—"

"How many men do you think would collapse if we maintain this speed?"

"T-ten?"

"A hundred at the most."

"So, you are aware that many of your men are suffering."

Rodrigo was starting to get annoyed. He had been in a good mood, recalling the way Estella had been sleeping peacefully beside him the previous night.

He said, "What do you think will happen if we take our time and arrive at the capital late? The emperor could take it as a sign of treason and have us all killed."

Foolish woman. Her empathy is completely unnecessary. Rodrigo turned his back to her. He had seen Anneheine lowering her head, but he didn't care. He immediately got back on his horse.

"Move out."

At his command, the resting soldiers stirred, gathering their things and readying to march again. He wanted to get to the next camping ground for the night as soon as possible. He intended to see Estella as soon as he entered his tent.

Billian ran for it, carrying Roa. I guarded them as I deflected Gilther's attacks. As I had suspected, Gilther had failed his level test on purpose. His skills were outstanding. Judging by his swordsmanship alone, he was a step above Ada and Ayla.

"You know what, Estella?" Gilther asked over the clash of our swords.

Gilther struck with force. He was full of energy—but we had already been fighting for hours and had been tired out by the monsters earlier.

"What, that you're acting like a psycho?"

Gilther's lips spread into a smirk. Gilther, who took after Schubert, reminded me of a croissant baked with low-quality butter. It might look appealing at first, but not when inspected up close.

"Getting injured or dying during lessons won't cause any issues."

I knew this well. It was why I was concerned about taking

lessons with Gilther. I pushed his blade away and put some distance between us.

"Estella, hurry up!" Billian yelled some ways away, having put Roa down for a moment.

He should be running away and hiding if he has the time! As soon as this thought occurred to me, Gilther threw a bomb in Billian's direction, not missing the opportunity. *I should have smashed his wrist before he could throw it!*

I swung my sword at Gilther, trying to slow him down so that Billian and Roa could escape. However, he was already procuring more explosives. The sound of another bomb exploding erupted as our blades met with a clang. *I hope Billian safely escaped with Roa.*

"Are you insane? Do you want us all to die?" I howled, ducking away from Gilther's blade.

"Yes, that's exactly what I want. Oh! Except for me." Gilther's eyes were glinting dangerously.

He's not in his right mind. That sort of craziness needs to be beaten out of him. I had difficulty trying to stop Gilther, whether because I had been slacking off training or because he was extremely skilled. I was worried about Roa. Still, I couldn't turn to look behind me.

"Do you know how long I've waited for this day? I had to act like a total moron because of you."

This confirmed that Gilther had intentionally failed his test so that he could kill me.

"Why are you doing this?"

"I just hate you."

I felt the same way about him. Gilther backed off a few steps. It signaled an oncoming attack. I wavered between deflecting his sword and running away—what would he do? I sprinted, hoping I was headed in the same direction as Billian and Roa. *I'll get her to safety before I continue this fight.*

Gilther wasn't deterred. Unwilling to let me go so easily, he traded his sword for a long whip and more handheld bombs. Chasing me, he chucked bombs and cracked his whip. I was totally preoccupied with avoiding the unending string of explosives and whip attacks.

I'm a fool for only bringing a sword to a sword-fighting lesson.

I could see Roa and Billian in the distance. The hem of Roa's skirt was stained red. My heart sank. Even as I ran, I could clearly see Billian biting his lip.

In Estella's empty room, Rodrigo leisurely perused her belongings. It had all been thanks to marching despite Anneheine's request to rest. Thanks to them arriving at the campsite for the night much sooner, the soldiers could put up their tents and rest much sooner than usual. The same went for Rodrigo.

He was curious how Estella would react to his appearing in her room earlier than usual. He had taken a bath and looked over all the books stacked on her desk while waiting for her to return. Quite a lot of time had passed.

"Lady Estella's lesson is taking much longer than usual." Jane's voice sounded from outside the tent.

Rodrigo paused to eavesdrop.

"You're right. It's already way past dinner time. Do you think something happened in the monster forest?"

"No way. The teacher isn't back yet either, so the lesson is probably running long. We should pack some food and have it sent to her."

"You plan on going yourself?"

The two voices gradually died away.

"Lesson?" Rodrigo looked out the window. The sun had already gone down. "It's too late."

He wanted to see her. Jane spoke about bringing her food. Rodrigo smiled brilliantly. Without hesitation, he leaped out of the window and hid along a path that Jane was likely to pass by. Silently, he waited for her to appear. Soon, Jane walked by his hiding place with a basket full of food.

"I will take that to her." Rodrigo stepped out in front of

Jane, causing her to jump.

Instead of screaming, she ran at Rodrigo with a dagger. *As expected of a Kartina staff member, I suppose.*

Rodrigo laughed exasperatedly and said, "It's me, Rodrigo."

"Y-your Grace?"

Only then did Jane peer at his face through the darkness and hide her dagger behind her back.

"Give me the basket." Rodrigo told Jane that he had overheard her as he took the basket from her. "I will take it to her. As her lover."

"There will be others, though."

In other words, she didn't advise him to let anyone else see him.

"I'll be discreet, so don't worry." Rodrigo was confident.

Confident that he could call Estella away from anyone else without getting caught. Jane looked doubtful as she looked at him, but she held out the basket anyway. Rodrigo immediately employed his expert stealth skills.

He slipped through the dark quickly and quietly and arrived at the woods. Once in the monster forest, he gave up on his plan to stay hidden to deliver the basket to Estella secretly.

"What kind of psycho dares to hurt my lover?"

He might explode, he felt, as he spotted Estella—barely standing as she struggled to hold out her sword.

CHAPTER
FIFTY-THREE

Instead of being surprised by Rodrigo's appearance, I welcomed it. He was like a superhero, arriving on the scene at the right moment to save the day. Really, he was basically a superhero. He was someone who could take care of this difficult situation faster than anyone I knew.

"Who's this? Erhart? Why did you decide to grace us with your presence?" Gilther laughed.

The disposition that had just seemed like a croissant with low-quality butter turned into a trampled croissant.

"How nice not to have to introduce myself. No need to identify yourself," Rodrigo muttered darkly.

He sounded nothing like my Rodrigo, the one I was used to.

"It'd be a waste of time to kill you after introductions." Rodrigo drew his sword.

This was the Rodrigo who had gone berserk. *Can he control it now or something?*

"Wait a moment," remarked Rodrigo. "I have to check something."

Gilther exhaled a huff of laughter. He seemed to be under

the impression that Rodrigo was trying to avoid a fight, and I started to feel bad for Gilther. *Run. Now, Gilther. No one can stop Rodrigo when he's gone berserk.*

However, Gilther simply raised his hands casually, offering him all the time he needed. Rodrigo turned his back to him. He was practically ignoring Gilther now, but Gilther himself seemed interested in the two of us and was still smirking. Or he was just an idiot.

"Estella, are you hurt?"

He was a gentleman.

"I'm fine. But..." I shook my head.

Turning around, I saw Billian backing away, holding Roa tightly in his arms.

"My cousin was injured."

Roa had been hit by shrapnel.

"She needs to be treated immediately. Could you take her?"

"I cannot carry more than one person."

He clarified that he didn't intend to leave me behind. I could tell just by looking into his eyes.

"Is that the reason you've been out here all this time?" Rodrigo pointed at Gilther.

"Yes."

"You couldn't eat, either."

"Right."

"It's gotten dark, and you're sweaty."

"Do I smell?"

"And exhausted." Rodrigo wasn't talking to me.

I shut my mouth.

"I would like you to close your eyes for a moment." Rodrigo procured a handkerchief.

Unlike the one he had given me on the battlefield, this one was clean.

"I am not really in a good mood, Estella. I have no patience to be answering your questions right now."

Rodrigo stepped closer. He folded his handkerchief and tied it around my eyes. My vision was immediately blocked. I could sense Billian trying to get up as if to fight against Rodrigo. I raised my hand.

"It's all right, Billian."

"I apologize for being so late," he apologized unnecessarily and stood up.

I reached out and grabbed at his pants.

"Estella?"

"...Don't kill him."

I showed Gilther the biggest mercy I could afford.

"Ugh... You bastard."

"It looks like you still have enough energy to talk. Shall I cut open your mouth next?"

Roa squeezed my sleeve tightly. Apparently, this was a scene that was gruesome, even for the Kartinas. Gilther's screams only got more high-pitched, and his curses grew fouler.

"Rodrigo!"

Roa was crying. She was gasping for breath, trying to smother her sobs, but I was sure she was crying. I decided that it was time to stop him. *But will he listen to me when he's gone berserk?* I wasn't sure. *No, maybe he's not actually out of control.* I called out his name with all my might. There was a gust of wind and the smell of blood.

"You called me, Estella?"

Rodrigo was suddenly standing in front of me.

"Let's go home."

"Shall we?"

His tone was gentle and kind, completely different from when he cursed at Gilther. So much so that I felt myself relaxing.

"Let me wrap this up quickly." Rodrigo moved away. "I'm going to stop here because I don't have enough time. But this isn't over. Keep your guard up. You won't be able to die even if you want to."

A heavy thud followed, like a sack of flour hitting the ground. Rodrigo appeared to have thrown Gilther. The string of groans I had been hearing went quiet. *He's not dead, is he?*

"I did not kill him. You told me not to."

Rodrigo removed the handkerchief from my face. I blinked a few times. Rodrigo's blurry face came into focus. Rodrigo gave me a long, concerned look before speaking up.

"Where do you want me to take you?"

I took Roa by the hand and pushed her toward Rodrigo.

"Would you take this little lady safely to my room?"

"As you wish."

Rodrigo scooped Roa into his arms. She struggled a bit, looking scared, but once she looked at Rodrigo's face and he gave her a few reassuring pats, she wrapped her arms around him without complaint.

Ha, I guess his good looks worked on her.

"Make sure to bring the basket," Rodrigo told Billian.

I nodded at the hesitant Billian, gesturing for him to follow us. He picked up the basket full of food and hurried after me.

"I'm just going along because of the food basket." Billian's voice was much softer.

I asked Rodrigo to help me enter the manor without being seen. Stefan and Hela weren't home, and Kalen, Ada, and Ayla were so busy that it was unlikely for us to run into them.

However, if anyone saw Rodrigo and word got to them, my entire family would get up in arms.

Rodrigo's triumphant return from the war was happening soon, so I wanted to avoid any complications. He took a moment to think before disappearing with Roa in his arms. When he returned, Roa was nowhere to be seen.

"I left her with Jane. In your room," Rodrigo told me before I could even ask. "Can you stay here alone?" He was addressing Billian.

Rodrigo had tied Gilther up, so he wouldn't be able to come after us immediately.

"Of course, I can, Sir Erhart," Billian shot back, sounding offended that Rodrigo would even ask such a thing.

"No, Rodrigo. Take Billian with you first."

"To be frank, Estella, I am not in a very good mood. I am holding back so as not to frighten you. Can you please be considerate?" he added the last sentence in a whisper near my ear.

His lips were warm. He did seem really angry. I had no choice but to raise my arms and wrap them around Rodrigo's shoulders. He chuckled lowly and picked me up.

"He'll be back for you soon."

I was worried about Billian, but I had to remind myself that he, too, was a Kartina. Rodrigo muttered something. My vision went white before going dark. When I opened my eyes again, we were in my room.

"My Lady! What on earth happened?"

Jane was smart. She hadn't called for a physician and had been treating Roa's thigh herself. She had finished giving first aid and was cleaning the skin around it when I appeared, and she threw down her towel and ran toward me.

"I'm not quite sure myself."

"Let us talk about this once I bring your cousin."

Rodrigo was determined to hear the full story. I had a moment to consider what exactly to tell him.

Roa toughed it out as her wound was treated, not crying even once, even though she was still a kid. Jane was responsible for extracting the shrapnel, disinfecting the wound, and stitching it back up. Rodrigo offered to dull the pain with his magic, but Roa shook her head.

"Why not, Roa?"

"...He's an Erhart."

I took a deep breath. *Sure, the Erharts and Kartinas are enemies, but...*

Rodrigo put his hand on my shoulder. As I raised my head, he smiled at me.

"The Kartina ladies are very brave."

Rodrigo spoke gently as if he was trying to ensure Roa didn't feel bad about rejecting him. Roa hung her head low, and I was relieved when I saw her blushing. Roa couldn't accept the Erharts because of what she had been taught all her life, but she would come to like Rodrigo.

Wait, but why am I happy about that? Who cares whether or not Roa likes Rodrigo? Our relationship would be over once our contract was completed. However, I felt like a bride being glad that her little sister was getting along with her new brother-in-law.

Suddenly embarrassed, I pushed Rodrigo's hand away.

"Now, shall we have a conversation among adults?"

It was the middle of the night. I knew we wouldn't be sleeping tonight.

"...Please look into this teacher. Or should I ask Devlon?"

"This is a Kartina matter."

At my words, Rodrigo's expression hardened, eyes dark.

"I am here as your lover, not an Erhart. As your husband-to-be, to be precise."

"Thank you. You've been a big help. We wouldn't have made it out safely without you earlier."

I had been about to throw myself at Gilther to stop him.

Roa had been turning paler and paler. My life might not have been in danger, but I could have broken a bone or lost a limb, or even more than that. Rodrigo's appearance had been miraculously timed, and I couldn't help but fall for him. Still, that didn't mean I could continue asking for his help.

"I am happy that you are willing to help, but your involvement will make things more complicated."

Gilther's attack on us might even look justified. Just because an Erhart had helped us.

"Estella..."

"Please do not underestimate us. We were simply caught off guard earlier."

Roa must have fallen asleep because Billian approached us. His tired face betrayed his young age. He had grown taller, but he was still just a boy. My heart felt heavy thinking about Billian having gone through this misfortune.

"You should rest."

"You need it more, Estella."

It was so strange to hear him call my name. *What's gotten into him?*

"Gilther didn't just plan this overnight."

Billian dragged over a chair and sat down next to me. Rodrigo looked at him, encouraging him to continue.

"For years now, Gilther has..."

CHAPTER
FIFTY-FOUR

"For years now, Gilther has hated you, Estella."

I wondered whether Billian was trying to insult me by mentioning a fact that was very clear to me already or whether he was trying to warn me. Unable to fathom his intent, I frowned and waited to hear more.

"Gilther didn't try anything until now because you've been lying low."

Lying low and behaving myself. It wasn't because of Gilther.

"But now..." Billian trailed off and glanced at Rodrigo. "He must have gotten angry because you got involved with the Erharts and started to get noticed by the imperial family as well."

"What, is he jealous or something?"

Both Rodrigo and Billian pulled a strange face at my question. I took a sip from the tea Jane had served us.

"Estella, Gilther is after the title of Count Kartina."

I snorted almost automatically. Even without me in the picture, Gilther was no match for Kalen. My brother was silly and childish around me, but not to anyone else. I almost pitied

Gilther for having such a foolish dream.

"That's what Uncle Schubert wants as well."

"What about you?"

I was suddenly curious as to why Billian acted friendly and shared all this information with me.

"I..." Billian took a deep breath. I could see a flash of fear cross his face. "I just want to live, Estella."

It was the first time I had seen my cousin's true face after fifteen years of knowing him, and it was pitiful and sad.

With a cat's stealth, Rodrigo took Billian home. We had agreed to tell people that Roa was so excited to see me that she would stay with me for a few days.

"Will you really not pursue this?" Rodrigo expressed his dissatisfaction with my decision not to punish Gilther.

I wiped away the little beads of sweat forming on Roa's forehead before standing up. Rodrigo's silhouette, as he leaned against the window frame, threw a dark shadow across the room. The sun was already rising. A chilly early morning breeze billowed through the open window and ruffled his hair.

"I will wait until after the celebrations in your honor are over," I said. "I won't do anything until then. Please don't make me repeat myself."

I could take care of my own affairs. And it was much better to use this against Gilther to pressure him instead of making a big deal out of it immediately. Killing each other to earn the title of successor was not uncommon among the Kartinas, after all.

"So all you need me to do is return and reach the capital as soon as possible by riding day and night?" Rodrigo sounded supportive, but he also didn't hide the frustration in his voice.

"Rodrigo, you should arrive on the date you're supposed to."

The date the emperor had set. He knew full well what going against that would mean.

"Do not make me strain myself," Rodrigo said sternly, and he glanced out the window.

The sun had nearly emerged fully from behind the mountains in the distance. It was time for Rodrigo to leave. Before he could use his magic, I held his hand. His eyes widened at the sudden touch.

Seeing how he suddenly relaxed was a relief, making him unrecognizable as the man who had just been driving such a hard bargain that he had seemed immovable.

"Rodrigo, don't strain yourself because of me."

His heart was set on me. As with all such epiphanies, the thought came out of nowhere. And it was weighty.

"You are the one causing me to strain myself. It would be

best not to continue this conversation today. It is making me more tired by the minute."

Rodrigo then slipped his hand out of mine. And suddenly, he was gone. The curtain fluttered in the spot where he had just stood. I could still feel his warmth in my hand, but my heart felt empty.

"Estella?"

She must've woken up at some point because Roa called me. I moved to stand beside her and feel her forehead. Smiling gently, I pulled the blanket up to her chin.

"Get some rest, Roa."

"What about you? Sleep next to me."

I wondered whether it was all right for me to go to sleep when Rodrigo hadn't slept a wink. However, denying myself sleep out of guilt won't change anything. I wrapped my arms around Roa and closed my eyes. I only realized that I had never cleaned myself up much later when Ayla and Ada returned home and screamed at the sight of me. My plan to cover up Gilther's attack failed.

"I'm going to kill that bastard!"

I could barely stop Ada from storming out the door with her sword.

"Ada, please hear me out."

"I heard he's seeing a girl these days," Ayla muttered menacingly.

"Ayla, please."

I knew too well what happened when villains attacked the people close to whom they wanted to antagonize. Rodrigo was living proof.

"How dare he lay a finger on you! And you want us to let that go?"

"Please hear me out. I will never let him get away with this. I'll get my revenge. But now isn't the time."

I finally managed to calm my sisters down. I had to promise to go to a popular teashop in the capital with them for them to listen to me. They finally sat down.

"I'm sorry, but Jane, could you take care of Roa?"

I ordered Jane to take Roa to her room in case Ada and Ayla said something drastic in their fury. Jane immediately followed my orders.

"Is this because of Rodrigo? That damn Erhart," Ayla said, grinding her teeth as Roa left the room.

I didn't respond. My sisters sighed simultaneously.

"Why are you playing it so safe?" Ayla and Ada looked at me in bewilderment.

From their perspectives, the careful moves I was making

were not smart. That was what it meant to grow up in the Kartina family.

Do not care about others. Do not forgive slights against you. Do not show mercy to anyone. Because we are Kartina.

However, I knew this was only possible when the Kartinas were on good terms with the imperial family. Since I had decided to marry an Erhart, the imperial family's favor would not last any longer, and we had to survive in our own way. I wanted to wait and observe the situation. Still, I wouldn't stand still. I looked at my sisters.

"We have to find that teacher first," I began. "Since I'm not very good at that, could you help me?"

"Of course. Shall we bring him here?"

"Yes, that would be great."

"Which part of him do you want? An arm, a leg, or his head?"

I bit my lip, shaking my head. "All of them in one piece, if possible. So he can breathe and talk, please."

"So he won't need his eyesight."

Ada and Ayla grinned. I wasn't sure whether I should be happy that they were so single-minded.

The blood-red curtain fluttered in the emperor's hall, quiet and tense. Emperor Thereo had sent away all his knights and officials. He sat, waiting, on a large plush couch. Repeatedly, he glanced over at the large door, waiting for someone. He tapped his foot and rubbed his fingernails. The fingernail on his thumb was particularly shiny, polished from rubbing it the most. Soon, without any warning, the large door opened, scraping against the carpet.

"Welcome, Your Holiness."

Thereo had leaped to his feet but sat back down when he saw the knights in the hallway peeking inside. Nathaniel was as beautiful as ever. The door closed behind him.

"Rodrigo's powers have awoken completely."

"I doubt it, Your Holiness."

Nathaniel began speaking as soon as he sat down, skipping over any greetings. Though the fact that he led with this news made it seem urgent, his voice was so calm and nonchalant that Thereo thought Nathaniel was joking about this serious matter.

Nathaniel's eyebrows shot up. His noticeably red lips formed a thin line.

"You seem to assume I would joke about such matters, Your Majesty."

Nathaniel's twisted smile was so cold that it could make even the most accomplished knights shudder. Even for Thereo, who had gone through all kinds of hardships and battles, it felt as though his insides were crumpling in on themselves.

"Imagine if his marriage to a Kartina goes through at this juncture. The empire will no longer belong to you, Your Majesty." Nathaniel rose to his feet.

"What would you have me do, Your Holiness?"

Nathaniel shrugged. "What do you think would be best? Are you not smart enough to think for yourself?"

Nathaniel left the hall without so much as a goodbye. Thereo, who had been staring at the doors in a daze, rubbed his face a few times and cursed.

"That damned bastard of a pope! Spitting on the temple would be a waste of spit!"

He could growl all he wanted, but ultimately, Thereo could do nothing but bow down to Nathaniel. That was how the imperial family had persisted thus far, even though they lacked talent. Still, this time, he had to do something. Thereo deliberated for a long time.

It was around the time that the sun, which had just reached its zenith, was starting to move west.

Imagine if his marriage to a Kartina goes through. That is what Nathaniel had said.

Thereo realized it was his way of saying he should stop this marriage. He rang the bell. His secretary, who had been on standby, quickly entered and bowed to him.

He told him, "Call for Count Kartina."

The victory celebrations were now only a day away. During the last few days, Rodrigo had been coming to see me in my room every night. We had gotten so used to each other that I was no longer startled when he showed up.

"Hello."

"I am late," Rodrigo said, who had indeed shown up later than usual, before announcing he would borrow my bathroom and disappearing inside it.

I sighed. After the incident with Gilther, it was hard to face Rodrigo. I didn't tell him about Ada and Ayla going to capture the teacher because Rodrigo didn't continue to ask what I would do about Gilther.

It was frustrating. *It would be nice to be able to work out and sweat it out.* Considering this, I selected a sword and pulled it from the wall. Its weight wanted to drag my arm down, but I swung it a few times. The muscles I had neglected to use while hiding my abilities tingled. They begged me to use them just once, so I stepped lightly and moved the practice sword. I was dressed only in my nightgown, so my movement wasn't restricted, and my swings increased. I leaped around the room, thinking of the chairs and tables as my enemies.

"Hm, do you hate me that much?"

I stopped dead, my sword's blade halting just below Rodrigo's chin as he emerged from the bathroom.

"I believe it's the opposite," I said.

He stared at me. Water droplets dripped from his wet hair.

"You believe I hate you?"

"Don't you? You don't talk to me, you don't get on the bed until I fall asleep, and then you're gone before I wake up. I thought maybe it was because you hated me."

All of the things that had upset me lately came flowing out of my mouth. I couldn't help it. I turned my head away. *I must look like a lover who's upset by her partner's lack of attention.*

"Actually, it is the opposite," Rodrigo said after a long moment of staring at me.

"What?" I asked.

His eyes, two brilliant red flames, met mine.

CHAPTER
FIFTY-FIVE

Rodrigo's eyes blazed crimson. I felt like I would melt just from his gaze. I took a deep breath and stepped back. However, the distance between us quickly decreased.

"Do you even want to know how I feel?"

No, I don't. Yes, I do. No, I already know.

I knew how Rodrigo felt about me. Still, I wanted to pretend that I didn't.

"You seem eager to exercise. Would you like to make a wager?"

"What kind of wager?"

"If I beat you without using my right hand..."

"Yes?"

"...Please be honest with me."

"That's not a fair game. You're bigger than me, you have much more experience in combat, and you're stronger. You can even use magic."

"Hm, where is your confidence? Are you the same Lady Estella who said you would save me at the ball?" Rodrigo was provoking me.

However, I didn't want to be the kind of idiot who got into a losing game because they were provoked.

"I would like to use a dagger," I said.

"You may use throwing knives as well. But no poison."

Well, that's doable. I tried to remember a scene from the novel. *Was Rodrigo right-handed or left-handed?* It hadn't been specified in the novel, but the promotional illustrations of him had depicted him holding his sword in his right hand.

I readjusted my grip on my dagger and swung it at Rodrigo's side. His eyes widened as if startled but soon turned into amused crescents.

He was still unarmed. I had deduced that it would be best to make him surrender before he could use a weapon. Unfortunately, Rodrigo was too quick and successfully managed to get a hold of his sword amid my string of attacks. He lifted the blade to block my dagger.

Clang.

The blades connected. Rodrigo didn't have a practice sword handy, so he left the sheath on his sword.

"Why won't you attack?" I snapped.

Whenever I approached, he would step away to keep a certain distance between us. *I need to get closer so I can use my dagger!*

Rodrigo simply smiled instead of replying. This was nothing but a game, but seeing him continue to evade me made me want to win. *And he's only using his left hand! He's too good!* I was embarrassed at myself for saying that I would protect someone so strong.

My body started to heat up. I realized Rodrigo had yet to put on a shirt after emerging from the bathroom. It was strange to watch him fight with a sword wearing nothing but pants.

"You seem to be planning to wear me out, but I'm in great shape, you know," I shot at him as I aimed for his side.

He was open; I was sure of that. However, suddenly, Rodrigo grabbed me by the waist and threw me onto the bed.

"R-Rodrigo!"

"It is nice to hear that you're in great shape, but let us end it here today."

He took my wrists and pushed them down against the mattress. I tried to keep my grip on my dagger, but he pushed down so hard that I had to release it. As soon as I did, it was game over for me.

I squeezed my eyes shut. My eyelashes trembled. My heart thumped wildly. The fact that Rodrigo's body felt warm over mine was a small consolation. It made me feel like I hadn't been the only one fighting tooth and nail, which was comforting.

"Go ahead. Ask me what you want."

I wished he would back off. He released my wrists, and I made to push him away, but I lowered my hands when I remembered he wasn't wearing a shirt.

Leaning over me, he chuckled, saying, "Let us do it this way. We will ask each other questions and tell only the truth."

"That's not what we agreed on."

"It is more efficient. If we keep talking in circles, we will be here all night. Are you not tired from sleeping poorly lately?"

He knows I keep waking up at night? Just as Rodrigo had said, I hadn't been able to sleep well lately. I kept waking up throughout the night. It was because he made me nervous. Still, every time I woke up, the space next to me on the bed would be empty. That made it harder to fall asleep again, and when I finally did, I would wake up again soon after. My sleep pattern was a total mess.

"I was watching you."

Was he just pretending to sleep in front of the desk?

"Why did you approach me? What is it that you really want? Can a Kartina and an Erhart really not work out? What will I have to give up to have you by my side?" His questions became heavier as he continued.

I couldn't bring myself to open my eyes.

"Just one," I suggested.

"Pardon?"

"Let's just ask each other one question."

Rodrigo sat up. Only then did I open my eyes and sit up as well.

"I lost, so I'm not in a position to negotiate, but let's do that. It won't be any fun if we know each other too well, right?"

Rodrigo looked at me strangely, neither happy nor sad, before chuckling and nodding. "All right. Go ahead and ask, then."

"You first."

"Ladies first is what I was taught."

"That's nice, but I would like you to go first."

"Will you be able to handle my question?"

I pressed my lips together when he said this. He was being very forward. Not physically, but in the way he looked at me. It was overwhelming.

"...I'll go first, then."

I lost to Rodrigo yet again. I wonder if I would ever win against him. I took a deep breath. *What should I ask him?* Really, I wanted to know far too many things. Whether he had changed his opinion about my family after meeting me, when he started using magic, and why on earth he kept coming to my room...

Still, what I wanted to know most was...

"How do you feel about me?"

Rodrigo flinched. He seemed surprised by my question. I was surprised too. I didn't think I would ask such an emotional question. I had intended to ask how he felt about my family.

"I like you."

Blood rushed to my face.

"...I see," I finally replied after a while.

I never thought the word "like" could be so heavy.

"I've kept telling you, and I thought I was communicating it well, but it seems that it was not enough," Rodrigo added, but I didn't hear a word.

What about the Kartinas? Do you like me enough to forgive my family for all the atrocities they committed against yours? Selfish questions came to mind, but we had agreed to ask each other only one.

"Go ahead."

Rodrigo dragged a chair over to the bed and sat down. We were close enough for our knees to touch.

"To make it crystal clear, I like you. So how do you feel about me?"

You are my lifeline. It was the first thing that came to mind. However, I knew it wasn't the right answer.

I said, "I'm not sure."

"Didn't we agree to tell each other the truth?"

"I'm being honest."

I wasn't lying. Technically, I did like Rodrigo, but I wasn't sure if my affection for him was deep enough for me to give up on everything else. I still wanted Rodrigo to have mercy on the Kartinas and was doing my best for that to happen. *Would I be able to stay with him without that objective?*

I wasn't sure.

Rodrigo looked at me for a long time without saying a word. I hung my head and avoided his gaze.

He said, "...I understand."

A shadow came over me. He stood up and walked away somewhere. When he returned, he had put on the rest of his clothes, and his expression had become somber.

"I will return to my tent for tonight. We have much to prepare before entering the capital tomorrow."

Rodrigo turned away. I didn't stop him.

It was very late at night when Stefan was summoned to see the emperor. Stefan had already been in a terrible mood, and he was ready to bite someone's head off, no matter their status.

"His Majesty said that it was urgent." Thereo's messenger tried to rush Stefan.

"You cannot expect me to face the emperor looking like this." His voice was gentle, but the hint of murderous intent in his words made the messenger back off a few steps.

Stefan wondered just how urgent this matter was, considering it warranted sending a messenger via teleportation. Along with a sorcerer, at that. One thing was certain. It couldn't be good news. Stefan was sure the emperor needed someone to clean up the mess he had made.

If the emperor needed his help, he could wait. Stefan took his time getting ready.

"You are late, Sir Stefan." Thereo's eyebrows furrowed at the sight of Stefan's immaculate appearance.

He could feel his temper rising at the fact that Stefan was dressed as if attending a banquet when he had just been hunting monsters at the western border.

"I did my best to hurry. I did not realize how late it had gotten."

The sun was beginning to rise. Thereo had been unable to sleep as he had been waiting for Stefan. Stefan felt much better at seeing the dark rings under the emperor's eyes and the bulging veins on his face.

"Have a seat."

Stefan, who had been standing in the doorway, walked over to the plush couch and sat down. At a glance from Thereo, everyone else inside the emperor's room left.

"I have something urgent to discuss with you."

"That is what I expected."

"That will simplify things."

As if things had ever been complicated. The emperor had a terrible habit of discussing difficult matters as if they were simple. Then again, being the emperor meant that he never had to worry about the details.

"Go ahead, Your Majesty."

Stefan acted like a loyal subject in front of the emperor. In truth, he had no respect whatsoever for Thereo. The emperor was simply a tool for making the Kartinas' lives easy. An irreplaceable tool.

"Get rid of Erhart."

The order that came out of the emperor's mouth was entirely unexpected.

"We are constantly doing our best to do so."

Ever since Stefan had become head of the house, the Erharts had not been their enemy. It seemed unnecessary to order this. Stefan was always trying to get rid of Rodrigo, as if it were his ultimate goal in life.

"Not just keeping him at bay, I mean..." Thereo paused for a moment. "I want you to kill him."

Stefan's expression hardened ever so slightly. Still, it was only for a moment. He flashed a smile as he looked at Thereo.

"Do you not benefit from the hostility between the Kartinas and the Erharts, Your Majesty?"

Thereo's gaze wavered noticeably. "What do you mean?"

Stefan felt the urge to spit at Thereo's detestable face but held himself back.

"Never mind. More importantly, are you ordering me to kill the empire's archduke?"

"Yes."

"That would entail too great a risk to my family, Your Majesty."

"I shall have the crown prince marry your daughter."

"Ada? Or Ayla?"

"Estella."

Stefan forgot who he was talking to and grimaced. He barely managed to hold back an insult. He knew what the crown prince was like. From Stefan's perspective, Detheus was beyond trash. That made him easy to use, and Ayla or Ada could handle him easily, but he did not suit the naive Estella.

Estella was naive enough to claim that she would marry Rodrigo because she had fallen in love at first sight.

"I cannot allow that."

"Why not?"

"I will never let her get married."

Thereo's brows raised sharply and then fell again. A smirk twisted the corners of his mouth, but he subdued any further expression.

"All right, I suppose it cannot be helped. However..."

Stefan's eyes narrowed at the way Thereo backed off so quickly.

"...Would you be against it if it was something your daughter wished for?"

There was no way.

"You wouldn't be against my son if you approved of Erhart, no?"

Approve of him? Stefan wanted to deny it, but he had missed his chance.

"Get rid of Erhart. Before he marries your daughter, I mean. Remember that I am the one who is in the same boat as you, not Erhart."

This was why he couldn't simply dismiss Thereo. He ruled over the whole empire from his seat in this small imperial palace. He might not be a man of action, but he was second to none when it came to scheming and calculating. Since he was the emperor, he had access to a wealth of information as well.

"Go ahead and try to win my daughter's heart then, Your Majesty."

263

Thereo chuckled quietly as he watched Stefan leave the room.

We shall see. Will I win her heart or destroy it? That will depend on you.

CHAPTER
FIFTY-SIX

"W-what's this?" Devlon would rarely get flustered.

"What do you think? It's a victory celebration," Rodrigo said nonchalantly.

Devlon's eyebrows furrowed. "*This* is it?"

They had just returned from a difficult war. While they hadn't expanded the empire's borders, the winning side could demand compensation from the losing side, so the empire had certainly made a profit. Still, the victory celebrations that welcomed them were so meager that even soldiers returning from a defeat would be disappointed.

"Maybe he got the date wrong?" Devlon suggested.

Rodrigo snorted. His attitude suggested that he was being ridiculous, so Devlon shut his mouth.

"Since when did we care about victory celebrations?"

It was true. Rodrigo had been on countless battlefields since he was young and had led countless battles to victory, but the celebrations were never for him. The emperor would always make him arrive at the capital late with the excuse of tying up loose ends around the battlefield, so Rodrigo had never once partaken in a victory celebration.

This time, he had been ordered to return immediately, so it appeared that the emperor had never intended to celebrate his victory. Rodrigo clicked his tongue.

"It must be nice to have someone waiting for you, though."

Devlon's words brought Rodrigo out of his reverie. He looked ahead. There was a blindingly white carriage decorated in giant, colorful feathers. The gems encrusted all along the carriage shone brilliantly in the sunlight. Next to it was a large banner. It read, "The strongest army! Fly, Black Dragon!"

The tips of Rodrigo's ears turned red.

"Come on, hurry!" Estella shouted.

It was the best welcome he had ever received.

"What is all this?"

I had expected his gratitude, but Rodrigo must've still been upset about last night because his tone was curt.

"Victory celebrations, what else? I tried my best to make it nice," I replied casually.

"You seem to have prepared a lot."

Rodrigo turned to look behind him. He gestured toward the pile of gifts meant for his knights and his most distinguished soldiers.

"This is nothing."

Rodrigo nodded. I felt oddly pleased because he seemed to agree with me. At the same time, my disappointment with the emperor came rushing back.

How can he neglect all these brave soldiers after they went through so much? Honestly, I had gone out onto the streets early in the morning to see what preparations were being made for the victory celebrations. Still, the streets had been completely quiet.

There had been no decorations, nor had the streets been cleaned up. That was when I realized that the emperor had no intention of celebrating Rodrigo's victory. Apparently, he hated Rodrigo enough to risk being criticized for being jealous of any attention paid to Rodrigo.

Still, I hadn't expected grandiose decorations or fanfare, but he could have at least had people throw flower petals to celebrate the returning army. It wasn't as if that would have inflated Rodrigo's ego or anything.

I had decided to make my own preparations. I had to spend some of the money I had saved and hassle my household staff but seeing Rodrigo's ears go red made it all worth it.

This is how you're supposed to use wealth and power, you useless emperor. I quietly raised my middle finger toward the imperial palace. It was then that Rodrigo reached out and wrapped me in an embrace.

"Thank you."

His hands, holding onto me tightly, felt warm. I could feel his sincere gratitude. I raised my arms and hugged him back.

"My birthday is coming up."

I let him know my true feelings indirectly. The feelings I had failed to tell him about last night.

Stefan was troubled as he watched the manor's hustle and bustle that had started early in the morning. He was not pleased that Estella had woken up so early to prepare to celebrate Rodrigo's return. Thereo had ordered him to separate Estella from Rodrigo. He hadn't said anything else, but his silence had implied a threat.

Stefan didn't like Rodrigo one bit. It was hard to say exactly why he felt this way. Perhaps it was Rodrigo's very existence. *But if Estella wants him...* Stefan was in a dilemma.

Estella was his precious daughter, whom he loved dearly. No one else knew this, but Estella had been conceived when Stefan and Hela's relationship had completely hit rock bottom. It was thanks to Estella that they were able to keep their family together. And the child that was born always put her family first and was the loveliest person.

Estella was his perfect daughter. She might be lacking as

a Kartina, but she was the first ever Kartina with absolutely no greed or ambition, so his heart went out to her. Whenever Stefan and Hela asked her if there was anything she wanted, Estella had only ever smiled at them. She was different from Ayla, Ada, and Kalen, who were always asking for things like the best explosives or magic scrolls. When they had given Estella a whole armory, she had only smiled slightly and hadn't been happy. He had been worried about her because nothing seemed to make her genuinely happy.

And then she finally said that she wanted something. She hadn't given up on her love despite all her family's attempts at coming between them. He figured that, as her father, even if he couldn't wholeheartedly support her, he at least couldn't stand in her way. Stefan watched Estella's carriage exit the manor gates and made up his mind.

He wouldn't get in her way. However, he couldn't help her, either. It was the most he could do for Estella.

Estella watched as Rodrigo swiftly assessed his troops before heading to the imperial palace. Everyone had places to be except for Anneheine.

There was no other option. I had to take Anneheine with me to the Kartina Manor.

"Why is she here?" Ada asked, glaring daggers at Anneheine.

It made sense that she disliked Anneheine, seeing what her father had made me go through.

"It's a long story, Ada."

I hid Anneheine behind my back. My sisters looked like they were ready to strangle her.

"Didn't Rodrigo agree to take care of her?"

"Of course, Sir Rodrigo will come to get her later."

"I don't like that, either."

Kalen appeared at the end of the hallway. He looked a bit tired.

"Kalen?"

"I captured the swordsmanship teacher, Estella."

He walked up to me and planted a kiss on the top of my head.

"The swordsmanship teacher?"

Anneheine stood on her tiptoes behind me and attempted to butt into our conversation. I found that Anneheine really had no tact and acted without much consideration for others. And yet she was the female lead. *Maybe that is why she is the lead.*

"This is none of your business, Anneheine. Shall we go, Estella?"

I didn't ask where we were going. He was obviously keeping him in the torture chamber adjoining his room.

"Has there been any news about the Veloki Kingdom?"

Things needed to wrap up there so we could decide on where Anneheine would stay.

"I suppose they will only make a move once the emperor demands compensation."

I guess there has to be justification for things to get going. Hoping the emperor would demand an extravagant amount, I left Anneheine to Jane.

"Shall we, Kalen?"

Kalen held out his hand.

He wants to escort me even when we're at home. He's so sappy.

"Why are you two coming?"

Ada and Ayla followed us as I walked with Kalen, who whirled around and glared at them.

"N-no reason."

"We said we would let whoever catches him take care of him. Right?"

"And that was me! I was the one who found out where he was staying!"

"Nuh-uh, it's only thanks to my sleeping gas that we were able to capture him quietly!" Ada and Ayla shouted back at Kalen.

"Whatever. Our agreement was about whoever catches him, so stop it. You two are embarrassing."

"Hey!" Ayla and Ada exclaimed simultaneously.

However, Kalen coldly turned his back on them. Then he looked at me and smiled warmly.

"Let's go, Estella."

"I-I told you everytin'!"

As soon as the door opened, a strong scent of blood and a muffled voice greeted us. Each step we took was accompanied by a splash as we walked across the wet floor.

"Don't be shocked, Estella. I made sure he couldn't move so that he can't attack you again," Kalen whispered sweetly as he turned on the light.

A bloody chunk of meat was in the corner.

"Th-thday away!" the chunk of meat spoke.

As my eyes adjusted to the light, I could make out its shape. It was the swordsmanship teacher who had poured monster pheromone powder on me... Or at least, I assumed it was him. It was probably him. With his nose and jaw clearly broken, the man pressed himself up against the wall as if he was trying to blend in with the wall.

"Repeat everything you told me before."

"W-wha'?" His voice was so small that it was hard to differentiate it from a moan.

As Kalen approached him, the man flinched violently.

"Whose orders did you follow?" Kalen demanded.

"Gi-ter." *Gilther.*

"And who helped you?"

"Maje-y." *His Majesty.*

"He told you to kill her?"

The man shook his head.

"What, then?"

"Th-thcare her." *Scare her.*

"Scare who?"

His bloodshot gaze traveled over to me past Kalen's shoulder. *Me.*

"So, the emperor and Gilther are in this together?"

The man shook his head at my question.

"D-dunno."

"Watch your tone when you speak to her."

"Kalen!"

I managed to stop Kalen from punching the man's already mangled jaw. If he were hit one more time, he'd be dead.

"Can you prove that the emperor was aiding Gilther? Or did you witness it yourself? The two of them together?"

The man wailed pitifully. *I guess he didn't see it.* That meant there was no reason to keep him alive. There were plenty of other witnesses to confirm Gilther's crime. Specifically, Billian and Roa.

"I'll leave the rest to you, Kalen."

I turned away. This man most likely wouldn't die a quick death. I could have shown mercy, but even if I did, he would have been killed by the emperor or Gilther. It would probably be better for him to just die here instead of getting tortured again by them.

Clack.

As the door closed behind me, I thought I heard a scream.

I shook my head. I needed to confirm whether Gilther and the emperor were cooperating and if they were, I needed to find out why.

The emperor was a meticulous man. I had tried to find proof of his interaction with Gilther but came up empty-handed. In the meantime, Hela returned home after killing off the monsters in the western region.

"There will be a banquet in three days, Estella," Hela said when our whole family gathered for dinner.

"A banquet for what?"

CHAPTER
FIFTY-SEVEN

"What banquet?"

Not that it mattered. It was just a formality.

"I want to rest at home, Mom."

If I said I wanted to attend this banquet, it would mean three whole days of shopping alone. And with Hela, at that. *No, thank you.* I was planning to look further into the connection between Gilther and Thereo. However, if I were to attend the banquet, I would be at Hela's mercy. I tried not to hurt her feelings as I voiced my refusal to attend.

Hela perked an eyebrow at me. "It is to celebrate Sir Erhart's promotion."

"Pardon?" I raised my voice without noticing.

"Who is hosting it?"

"Sir Erhart."

He's holding a banquet without even telling me? But he told Hela first? He didn't say a word when I saw him this morning.

"I met him at the imperial palace this afternoon," Hela added at the sight of my expression hardening.

I felt awkward that she noticed and rubbed the tip of my

nose and fiddled with my spoon. I lowered my head and began to ruminate. About how long it had been since a banquet had been hosted at the Erhart Manor and about the reason for this sudden banquet when this wasn't the first or second time Rodrigo had led a war to victory. I had no idea my whole family was looking at me.

"Today's dinner is smoked duck with an apple yogurt sauce."

The chef came in to serve us dinner but flinched as he looked up and was met with five pairs of eyes. *I guess it's scary to have five Kartinas stare at you, regardless of whether they're being hostile.*

"What a wonderful dish," I said when everybody else remained silent.

Only then did the chef return to the kitchen. I poked at my food for a few minutes.

Looking between my family members, I asked, "Is there anything you want to tell me?"

Judging by how they were exchanging glances, tonight's dinner seemed to be some sort of family meeting.

"I'll allow it," Stefan said suddenly.

Everyone besides me looked abruptly like they were mourning the death of a loved one at their funeral.

"What exactly are you allowing?"

"Sir Erhart. But..."

"But?"

"You won't be getting any help from me." Stefan's voice trembled.

I couldn't think of anything to say because he sounded like an emotional father walking his daughter down the aisle.

"Not us. That stubborn bastard," Kalen added.

Did something happen with Prince Detheus?

"Erhart is at least better than Prince Detheus."

What is that supposed to mean? When I looked over at Kalen, he cleared his throat and began to tell me something completely ridiculous.

"That bastard kept hassling me to allow him to meet you. He was sending me over twenty messages a day at one point."

"Did you only get messages, Kalen? He sent me gifts too! Ha, I never thought I would be getting flowers from a man," Ayla said.

I was wondering why Detheus hadn't contacted me in a while. Apparently, he had been trying to gain my family's favor.

"Erhart is better than Detheus. At least he's capable, though I hate to admit it," Ada said.

"He's also much more handsome," I added.

Everyone grimaced, but it didn't stop me from rejoicing since I had even been thinking of precautions to take with their disapproval in mind. I had already felt terrible about the significant financial losses Rodrigo had to take due to my family's disapproval. I had given up on their blessing when I proposed to Rodrigo. I hadn't expected them to approve so easily. I was so pleased that I could have danced. *Is there anything I could do for them?*

I took a moment to think before speaking up again. "Ada, Ayla, would you like to sleep in my room tonight?"

My sisters looked at me as if they were on top of the world. I started to feel bad about having neglected them lately as I watched their eyes shine with unshed tears of happiness and their jaws drop slowly.

"Estella, my angel!" Ada threw her arms around me so hard that our chairs wobbled.

"Aaargh! Me too!" Kalen's hand shot up in the air.

"No boys allowed, Kalen," Ayla shot back immediately.

I felt bad. It would have been fine if we were still kids, but we are much older now. I was technically still a minor, but I was less than a month away from becoming an adult.

"My bed is quite large, too, you know," Hela mumbled.

She sounded like she was talking to herself but had spoken loud enough for us to hear, so I indulged her and reached out a hand.

"You too, mom!"

"W-what about me?"

Hela glared at Stefan. He avoided her gaze. His sad puppy-dog eyes were heartbreaking, but I decided to appease him by going on a walk through the gardens with him tomorrow.

"Oh well. At least allow me to sleep in the room next to Estella's, Hela," Stefan asked gently.

Hela nodded reluctantly. "You are the master of this manor, so suit yourself. However, we will be sleeping in my room, so do not make a racket."

Stefan also nodded reluctantly, and Kalen stuck to his side. It had been a while since dinner time had been so lively.

Someone softly caressed my hair as I listened to the even breathing beside me. Hela had given me a long-winded speech about the futility of love.

"I can't believe my baby has fallen in love. It brings tears to my eyes."

At the end of her speech, she told me she would support my relationship and hugged me tightly. I had fallen asleep in a great mood, but... I woke up to a racket.

The sound made my stomach turn even though I couldn't identify it yet. I grimaced. Hela had already woken up and was preparing to greet a guest.

"Mom?"

When I called her, she turned to look at me. A warm smile spread across her cold face. She stepped closer and stroked my hair.

"You can go back to sleep."

"Is somebody here?"

"There seems to be an unwelcome guest. Go back to sleep, honey." Hela planted a kiss on my forehead.

"Who is it?"

Maybe someone from Erhart Manor? I figured that even if they had given us their blessing now, someone from Erhart Manor wouldn't be a welcome guest so soon.

"Your uncle is here."

Oh, Gilther's father, Schubert. He was indeed an unwelcome guest. And it was true that I shouldn't get involved. I burrowed back beneath the covers. *I wonder what Kalen did to that teacher.*

Blanche grew deathly pale at the official demand for restitution that had arrived from the empire.

"T-this much?"

Just as Estella and Rodrigo had wanted, Blanche held Franz responsible for failing to govern properly and had taken the throne. It was a usurpation in name only because, technically, he had ascended the throne thanks to Rodrigo and Estella.

During this process, Blanche declared that the kingdom could no longer sustain this drawn-out war and announced its end.

Veloki had thus surrendered to the empire.

There had been a brief uproar in the kingdom, but just as Rodrigo and Estella had said, the kingdom's people weren't overly invested in the war. Only the nobles got busy figuring out which way the power would shift and changing sides accordingly. Thanks to this, Franz could very clearly differentiate between friend and foe. Franz had moved to a sparsely populated region on the kingdom's outskirts, and Blanche had taken the throne.

And a few days later, a request for restitution arrived from the empire.

"H-how could we possibly afford all this?"

It was a demand for Veloki to oversee the rebuilding of all the areas affected by the war and to relinquish some of the territories to the empire. There was also a demand for hundreds of young women and a thousand slaves. Though his reign was temporary, the fact that his first order of business as king was to arrange to pay restitution to the empire left a bitter taste in Blanche's mouth.

He considered going to the emperor and telling him that he was only a puppet and that Rodrigo was behind all of it.

At this point, it looked as though Franz would return to the throne and Blanche would be stoned to death by the masses after losing his royal status. However, Blanche couldn't do anything about it because of his daughter, Anneheine. The daughter he had worked so hard to have. Though she refused to acknowledge it, Anneheine was his daughter by blood. The only family he had left in the world. There was nothing he wouldn't do for her. Indeed, she was the reason he had worked with the mad sorcerer. Someone had told Blanche that he would take care of Anneheine and everything else if Blanche disposed of Rodrigo. Still, when things had gone south, he had disappeared, and he hadn't been able to contact him at all.

The only person Blanche could now rely on was Franz. Franz had guaranteed his and his daughter's safety.

Blanche clenched his fists. He couldn't sit idly by forever.

"Put together a team of messengers to send to the empire."

"Breakfast is ready," Augus announced as he knocked on Anneheine's door.

"One second!"

There was a loud commotion from inside. Augus frowned. He couldn't understand Rodrigo's decision to bring back the enemy's daughter from the battlefield. She was a hostage in name but didn't act like one. She strutted around the Erhart

Manor as if she owned the place and didn't hesitate to demand things from the household staff. She seemed to take the service for granted and even requested things that crossed the line.

"It would be best to plant roses in this garden. Shall we plant them next year?"

She was acting like the lady of the house. All the household staff at the manor, including Augus, were uncomfortable with this but did not show it. Although she was a hostage, Rodrigo had ordered them to treat her like a guest, and making a guest uncomfortable was unacceptable to the Erhart Manor staff.

"Could you bring the food to my room?" She still seemed unprepared as she shouted from inside.

Augus clicked his tongue. He couldn't help comparing her to Estella. Estella's manners were impeccable and overflowing with noble elegance, so much so that it was hard to believe she was a Kartina. There was a world of difference between her and Anneheine.

He wondered how Rodrigo's relationship with Estella was going. There were still a few more gifts that Rodrigo had instructed him to give to her. He decided to try and pry Rodrigo out of his room, where he had been since he had returned from the war and force him to go to her.

"Understood," Augus replied and told the staff to bring breakfast to Anneheine before going to see Rodrigo.

Rodrigo sat at his desk for hours, tapping his fingers on the hard wood, thinking. He was concerned about the conversation he had had with Thereo. It was unusual for him to call Rodrigo directly to his reception room as soon as he had returned from the war. He had given Rodrigo a pat on the shoulder and congratulated him on the victory. That itself was already surprising, but what followed was even more so.

"Since you are back now, all that's left is your wedding with Lady Kartina, isn't it?"

Rodrigo had expected the emperor to interfere with his plans somehow, but he had spoken as if he approved of everything.

"Detheus will be quite upset."

Rodrigo had stood there and listened.

"I suppose it's the way things should be. It simply wasn't meant to be."

The emperor had changed. He became extremely friendly. For the first time in his life, Rodrigo had seen the emperor be so kind to him. *What on earth changed?*

CHAPTER
FIFTY-EIGHT

Unable to gauge the intent behind the emperor's drastic change, Rodrigo shut himself inside the Erhart Manor. While there, he received a message from Duke Gloria congratulating him on his victory. Though he would have normally visited the duke immediately, Rodrigo only sent a short reply this time.

"Your Grace."

Augus came to see him. Rodrigo swiveled around in his chair from facing the window to turn to Augus.

"What is it?"

"What shall I do with the gifts I have yet to deliver to Lady Estella?"

"Why would you even ask?" Rodrigo raised his eyebrow. There was a growl to his voice. He got to his feet and headed toward the bathroom, saying, "Go get my clothes, Augus,"

"Are you going to deliver them personally?"

"Of course, I will. She's my lover."

"You seemed too busy to go by yourself."

"Augus." Rodrigo paused, his hand on the bathroom door. He turned to look at Augus.

"Yes, Your Grace."

"Estella is my highest priority. No matter how busy I might be, I want to tend to her myself. From now on, prioritize every matter related to her above all else. If I happen to be unable to go to her myself, you must go in my stead."

Augus bowed his head. He had been worried that Rodrigo might have been swayed by Anneheine, but his words were extremely reassuring.

"Yes, Your Grace. I shall prepare your clothes."

After this confirmation, Rodrigo stepped into the bathroom and shut the door.

A few days had passed since Schubert had visited. However, neither Stefan nor Hela would tell me why.

"What class do you have today, Estella?" Hela asked during breakfast.

"I have poison-making class today."

"All right. Is it not too difficult to take classes with your young cousins?"

This was the second time we would take a class together. Since Gilther had completely ruined the first lesson, it was hard to gauge whether it was difficult to take a class with my cousins.

"It's all right."

There were only so many things I could say. Hela and Stefan looked at me with concern.

"If you don't feel comfortable taking classes with them, I could give you private lessons. You'll get to the next level in no time."

"It's all right, Mom. You're busy enough already. I will take my time and do my best to get through this on my own!"

As I watched Hela's eyes fill with proud tears, I changed the subject.

"Oh my, the fresh scallop salad is so delicious today."

"Really? Have some more."

Hela ladled another scoop of scallop salad onto my plate. I immediately took another bite. Hela and Stefan put down their forks to watch me eat as if that was enough for them to feel full. Their lips formed gentle smiles.

"If you don't like the teacher or he bullies you, you must tell us immediately."

I felt a prick in my conscience. *Did Schubert visit to talk about what Gilther did? No. There's no way.* I knew Schubert well enough to know he would never volunteer any information that might put him in a bad light.

"O-of course."

"Or if your younger cousins bother you."

"All right."

"Or your older cousin."

"Pardon? My older cousin?"

"I mean Gilther. Although I understand that he does not act older in any way."

What are they saying? I thought Gilther was only taking sword-fighting classes with me.

"Gilther will be there too? For the poison-making class?"

Hela grimaced as she nodded. "Apparently, that complete fool cheated during the test. His test was voided, and now he has to take classes with you."

"He's an embarrassment to the Kartinas. I would love to forbid him from even setting foot inside the manor, but I had no choice after Schubert came to ask me to allow it." Stefan chewed violently on a piece of an apple as if he imagined it was Gilther or Schubert.

Oh, so that's why Schubert was here. Gilther had to retake poison-making lessons because he had failed his test, and it was too expensive to look for a tutor, so Schubert must have come to my family so Gilther could join us. *But wasn't he just fine on his own before?* I had a bad feeling about this as I recalled the sword-fighting lesson.

"Is he starting today too?" I asked carefully.

I would be fine, but I was worried about Roa and Billian.

"He seemed to be in a hurry. He will start classes today."

Oh great. Does he have the poison-making class teacher in his pocket too? I finished my plate, planning to find out as soon as possible.

"You'll be taking classes with Gilther?"

When I returned to my room, I called for Ayla, Ada, and Kalen. My siblings left behind whatever they were doing without hesitation. Judging by how out of breath they were, they must have run all the way to my room. To thank them, I served them tea as I relayed what Hela had told me.

"That's right."

"I can't let that happen. I must go and tell father what happened last time!" Kalen exclaimed.

My sisters managed to stop him from running off.

"Why not? The victory celebrations are over."

"This could be related to the emperor, you said," Ayla reminded him.

Kalen nodded.

"But the other teacher died."

Oh no, he must have died from all that torture. Kalen lowered his head as if he were acknowledging his mistake. Ada and Ayla began to criticize him for being a fool.

"Stop it."

I took Kalen's side. It was a miracle he didn't kill the man immediately. I knew Kalen had held back.

"Well, do you two have a plan, then? Gilther, that scum, will be spending half a day with our dear Estella! If he's joining her for both classes, that's twice a week. Twice a week!" Kalen was shouting.

His eyes began to go bloodshot, so I took a firm hold of his sleeve before he could explode.

I hoped that my small gesture would help him calm down. Kalen slumped into a chair with a loud thud.

"Should I hand in my advancement badge?" Ada said.

Ayla and Kalen's eyes widened.

"What are you saying, Ada!" I immediately objected.

If you failed even one subject, you couldn't go on missions as a Kartina. Unlike me, Ada, Ayla, and Kalen felt a sense of achievement from accomplishing missions as Kartina agents, and that was their joy in life. I couldn't make them give that up just for me. Even though they were villains.

"What should we do?"

My siblings put their heads together to contemplate this problem. The reason I told them about this wasn't because I wanted them to give me a solution. I had only told them in case they found out later and did something drastic, but it seemed

I had made the wrong choice. Watching their expressions darken made me feel sorry for them.

"What is the meaning of all this?"

Just then, I heard Rodrigo's voice. I had no idea how long he had been there, but Rodrigo's voice was stern and thick with fatigue. He hopped off the windowsill.

"Rodrigo?"

"Yes, Estella. It's me."

He didn't miss so much as a beat and came straight over to me to kiss the top of my head. My siblings raised their heads in obvious disapproval, but Rodrigo didn't pay them any mind.

"You're taking classes with Gilther, Estella?" he asked.

"How much did you hear?"

"Since Kalen tried to storm off."

So everything. Why are you asking, then? I said, "Yes, it turned out that way."

"Is there no way to change this?" Rodrigo asked Kalen.

Kalen shook his head. It had been Stefan's decision. Unless we defied Stefan, there was no way to change this.

"I shall meet with the count."

"What do you plan to tell him?" Kalen seemed delighted.

I guess he doesn't think I can stop Rodrigo.

"I will tell him everything about what happened that day during the sword-fighting lesson."

"Wow, Sir Erhart. Not bad." Kalen didn't hold back his praise for Rodrigo's plan.

"You can't, Rodrigo. Are you trying to start a war inside the capital?" I couldn't help but interrupt them.

"A war?"

"Do you think my father will let this go? He will start an outright war against Schubert."

"Is Schubert that strong?" Rodrigo gave me a confused look.

He was asking whether Schubert had enough forces even to start a war. I was happy to hear that he thought highly of our forces, but he forgot that Schubert, too, was a Kartina. Though he had failed to obtain the title of count, Schubert had also acquired quite a fortune by using the skills he had acquired as a Kartina. In other words, his forces were formidable as well.

If we went for a frontal attack, Stefan would win without a doubt. Still, that didn't mean that our family would get away without any casualties.

"Don't forget that Schubert is a Kartina, too," I replied simply.

Rodrigo immediately understood what I meant. *Smart man.*

"Let us clarify what you want," Rodrigo said as he sat beside me.

Jane brought out another teacup, and I poured some tea for him.

"What I want?" Estella asked.

Rodrigo nodded.

"You do not want to go to war against Schubert. Right?"

"Yes, that's right."

"Roa and Billian, was it? You don't want them to get hurt, either," Rodrigo said.

"Of course not," I said.

"You fighting against Gilther... might be a bit difficult." Rodrigo stroked his chin.

He knew full well that I wouldn't back down from a fight. I cleared my throat.

"What do you mean? Estella fighting Gilther? My little Estella couldn't hurt a fly," Kalen said, clicking his tongue.

Rodrigo grinned. "Is that so?"

And then he looked at me. I avoided his gaze.

"All right. So fighting against Gilther is out of the question as well. Then we only have one other option." Rodrigo held up one finger.

"And what's that?" Kalen grimaced as he asked.

Everyone looked at Rodrigo, who grinned again.

CHAPTER
FIFTY-NINE

"I will join her class."

There was a round of snorts that went around the room. I didn't want to laugh at him, but his suggestion was in no way viable.

"Can't I?" He tilted his head, confused by our reactions.

"Are you being serious, Sir Rodrigo?" Kalen muttered something about a useless fool.

"Kalen," I called his name warningly.

Kalen was dangerously close to crossing a line. When I glared at him, Kalen flinched and raised a hand.

"That was rude of me."

"It's all right. You are Estella's dear brother, after all. Otherwise..." Rodrigo smirked.

He was still beautiful, but that smirk was chilling.

"I need an explanation as to why not, Estella." Rodrigo turned toward me.

I could smell his familiar scent as he leaned closer.

"The Kartina curriculum is top secret since we're taught secret techniques. Not only are you from a different family, but teaching you secret techniques won't benefit us. You may even use them against us."

"Even though I'm going to be part of your family soon?" Rodrigo reached out and wrapped his arm around my waist.

Hey! I swatted at his hand, but Rodrigo just smiled. He often initiated public displays of affection like this as if to show others we really were madly in love. He would smile sweetly at me and talk to me in a loving voice, and when he looked at me with eyes that seemed genuinely in love, it was impossible to keep my heart from fluttering.

Then again, I suppose Rodrigo had confessed that he did like me.

"Hands off," Ada commanded.

"I apologize." Rodrigo immediately pulled away and put both hands in the air.

"What do you mean you'll be part of our family?"

"Before I left for the war, Countess Hela gave me a promise that she would approve our marriage when I returned. And I have already proposed to Estella and will do so."

"Have already proposed and will do so?" Ayla asked.

"I just put a ring on her finger, you see."

What? Startled, I raised my hand. Just as Rodrigo had said, there was a pink diamond ring sparkling on my left ring finger.

"And I will propose to her officially on her birthday. You

will be holding a banquet, right?"

My siblings all pursed their lips simultaneously. They wanted to object, but they knew very well the value of the diamond on my hand, so they didn't say anything.

"So, now that it's been decided that I will be joining your family, may I participate in this class?"

"Well..." Kalen seemed conflicted.

"I suppose it would be possible if mother allows it," Ayla said.

Rodrigo immediately got to his feet and went over to Hela's office. He returned triumphantly.

"Let's go to class, Estella."

Nobody knew how he had convinced Hela. Rodrigo refused to tell me, no matter how many times I asked.

"It may be difficult for you because you haven't built up a tolerance for poisons," I told him as we walked toward a building on the western side of the manor grounds.

Rodrigo smiled widely and leaned down. His scent reached me first, and then his breath tickled my ears.

As I raised my shoulders and shivered, Rodrigo chuckled and said, "Magic has many uses."

"You mean you can use it to neutralize poisons?" I asked, shocked.

Rodrigo just grinned without saying a word. I was reminded yet again of how amazing magic was. At the same time, I felt a bit annoyed at the many years I had spent building up a tolerance against poisons. Some people could apparently neutralize poison without any trouble, while I had to spend my childhood adding increasing amounts of poison to my food. *Unfair.*

"It isn't perfect yet, but I doubt they will give me enough poison to kill me."

"They might."

Rodrigo looked a bit more serious as he stroked his chin.

"That is troubling. How could I die without you? I could never."

He's such a sap! I lightly elbowed him in the chest.

"Argh!" He bent over.

I didn't put any strength into it... but maybe I did? Frowning, I asked, "Are you all right, Rodrigo?"

"I c-can't breathe."

"Oh no, really?" My chest tightened. "What do we do? Can you do something with magic?"

What do you do when someone can't breathe? I tried to remember all the first aid I had learned while picking up after the Kartinas' misdeeds, but nothing came to mind. My mind was completely blank.

"Rodrigo, Rodrigo!" All I could do was call his name repeatedly. "Can you walk at all? I'll hold you."

I slipped underneath his torso and tried to straighten him up by the shoulder. Suddenly, Rodrigo straightened up and trapped me in his arms.

"...Rodrigo?"

His breath was even. When I looked up to face him, I saw that his face looked completely fine too. The tightness in my chest released.

Then I snapped, "You were making fun of me?"

"You seem to be worried about me."

"What? Are you being serious right now?" I raised my voice. "Let go of me this instant!"

I twisted around in Rodrigo's embrace. He didn't budge even as I clenched my fists and hit his sides. It was because I didn't hit him hard—just in case I had actually hurt him earlier. Rodrigo held me tighter.

"You haven't told your mother that."

"Don't change the subject."

"I thought it was strange. To hear that that bastard—I mean, Gilther—was going to take more classes with you. What were you thinking?"

I realized Rodrigo was angry at me.

"My victory celebrations are over, and the emperor even

complimented me. You said you did not want to start a war, but I am confused about whether you are doing this because you really do not wish for war or because of me."

I sighed. Rodrigo must have been shocked just as much as I had been by Gilther's attack. He was as worried even more than I was worried about him. It made my heart flutter.

Quietly, I told him the truth, "Gilther has a connection to His Majesty."

"The emperor?"

Rodrigo's arms loosened around me. There was a small gap between us. I looked up to face him. He looked down at me. His red eyes reflected only on me.

"Yes."

"Any evidence?"

"None. And the witness died," I admitted.

Rodrigo's expression darkened.

"Don't worry. I'll get to the bottom of it."

"Do you think that is what I am worried about?"

"Don't worry about me, either," I told him, taking the opportunity to escape his embrace while his guard was down.

He smiled dejectedly at the space between his arms and shook his head.

"How could I not worry?"

"Do you not trust me?" I asked.

"I do. So much. But…"

"But?"

"The emperor is not an easy foe."

"Oh? Are you jumping to conclusions without evidence and saying that the emperor is after me by working with Gilther? That's a stretch."

"It was strange, you see."

What is he talking about? As my eyes widened, Rodrigo stepped closer to me. As if he was making sure no one would overhear.

"As I mentioned earlier, the emperor praised me," he said.

"Of course, he did. You won the war."

"He has never done so before."

He was saying that the emperor had changed. And the timing was suspiciously close to Gilther coming after me.

"You cannot ignore even the smallest detail, Estella," Rodrigo said.

"Are you giving me advice?"

"Let us say that I am sharing what I learned from my life experience."

Visions of his devastating past flashed through my memory. Rodrigo noticed my expression darken and caressed my cheek.

"Do not worry," he said, brushing his fingers gingerly across my skin. "I will protect you no matter what."

My eyes widened. "Rodrigo, how many times do I have to tell you that it's the other way around? You're the one who shouldn't worry. I will protect you."

"How reassuring."

Rodrigo and I laughed for a long time as we faced each other.

"We'll be late at this rate." I took Rodrigo by the hand and pulled him along.

Rodrigo's hand was warm, and mine was cold. Together, they became the perfect temperature.

"H-huh?" Billian's first reaction to seeing Rodrigo was decidedly negative.

"Oh! It's the man who carried me!" Roa, on the other hand, smiled broadly.

She reached out her arms and ran over to Rodrigo. He easily caught her with one arm and picked her up.

"What about me?" I complained, disappointed by her welcome.

Roa covered her mouth with her small hands and giggled.

"He's so big that I didn't even see you."

Rodrigo is very big. Since I was standing behind him, it made sense that... No, that doesn't make sense! My dress skirts would have been totally visible! I pinched Roa's little nose and twisted it lightly at her cute excuse. Roa just grinned. She seemed to have forgotten all about her discomfort with Rodrigo being an Erhart.

"Are you insane, Estella? He's an Erhart!" Billian approached and glared at me.

"That's right. Rodrigo is an Erhart. And he's the one who saved you, me, and Roa."

"And I'm thankful for it... I'm going to send a thank-you gift."

"That's all right. I'll consider it received," Rodrigo added.

Billian took a step back. He seemed annoyed that he had to look up at Rodrigo when he was standing close by.

"I learned that favors should be returned."

"You're wrong. You were taught to pay your enemies back double," I said.

"That's the same thing, Estella." Billian puffed out his chest as if to tell me not to butt in.

"Is that really what you believe, Billian?" A low, baritone voice called out.

We all turned toward the door. Gilther was watching us, leaning against the doorway and dressed neatly.

"G-Gilther!" Billian's shoulders drooped as he called out to Gilther.

Did something happen between these two? Billian seemed overly frightened of Gilther. Then again, I remembered that I hadn't had the time to check up on Billian and Roa after the incident.

Maybe Gilther had gone to see them and made a fuss.

"More importantly, an Erhart? Billian, if you meet an Erhart, you should be throwing a knife immediately, not standing there making conversation."

Before he even finished his sentence, Gilther threw a dagger. It wasn't aimed at Rodrigo—it was aimed at me.

CHAPTER
SIXTY

I wondered whether the dagger Gilther had thrown while insulting the Erharts was aimed at me by chance or on purpose. I was ready to bet that it was the latter.

"It seems as though we must see blood today," Rodrigo muttered as he pulled me out of the way.

The dagger whizzed past the spot I had been standing in and embedded itself in the wall behind us. Rodrigo glared at Gilther with Roa in one arm and me in the other.

"Oops, my hand is slippery," Gilther said, sounding not at all sorry as he took out another dagger.

However, he didn't have the chance to throw it because Rodrigo moved up to Gilther in the blink of an eye, letting go of Roa and me, and was pointing his sword at him.

"I do not make idiotic mistakes like letting daggers slip from my hand."

"There must be something wrong with your head. We're in Kartina territory. And you're an Erhart," Gilther snapped. He turned to his cousin, saying, "What are you waiting for, Billian? I, a Kartina, am being attacked by an Erhart."

Billian reached into his pocket and withdrew a bottle of poison he had prepared for today's class.

"That's right. Good job, Billian. I keep telling you. If you want to be a Kartina, you have to prove yourself. Now is your time. Go ahead and throw it."

I knew Rodrigo could knock away a poison bottle or avoid it easily, but I was worried about what would happen next. I grabbed Billian's wrist. His wavering gaze turned toward me.

"I am going to marry that man soon. In other words, he will become part of the Kartina family." *So there's no need to attack him right now.*

"What do you mean, Estella? Ah, yes, I did hear you were busy playing around these days. But do you really intend to marry an Erhart?" Gilther hissed.

He was trying to provoke me. *I'll rip out his tongue and wrap it around his face.*

Looking away from him, I reached out and snatched the poison bottle from Billian, saying, "I just stole this bottle from you. Do you understand?" I pushed him toward Roa.

"You talk too much. Aren't we Kartinas about actions rather than words?" Rodrigo muttered menacingly.

I grit my teeth, trying to steal a moment to think. *Should I let Rodrigo kill Gilther?* I really wanted to, but behind Gilther was a much bigger fish. I concluded that until I could find his connection to the emperor, he had to stay alive.

"Rodrigo, this is Kartina territory."

"Do Kartina cousins always throw daggers at each other?"

I nodded. Rodrigo frowned. *Of course, he doesn't get it.* However, it was true. To get the title of Count Kartina, throwing explosives, let alone daggers, at each other was commonplace.

"What, are you disappointed in our family? Or are you scared?" Gilther blathered like a schoolyard bully.

Ugh, I just want to... I called, "Come here, Rodrigo."

Rodrigo did not lower his sword as he began to pat down Gilther. He had all kinds of poison bottles, throwing knives, and even a longsword. Rodrigo removed them all and tossed them far away. Gilther raised his hands as if to surrender, and Rodrigo clenched his jaw. I could tell just how angry he was by the vein pulsing along his jawline.

"I am only holding back because of you, all right?" Rodrigo said.

"I know. Thank you. You have to hold back because you are an Erhart. I, however..."

I took off one of my heels. As I stepped down from my high-heeled shoes, Rodrigo became even taller. Well, technically, I became shorter.

Rodrigo's eyes were asking what on earth I was doing.

"You have to hold back, but I don't." I smiled at him and

threw my shoe at Gilther.

I wanted it to knock that filthy grin off his face. The heeled shoe zipped through the air in a straight line. Startled, Gilther raised his hand to swat it away, but suddenly a gust of wind came blowing in and changed its trajectory.

Rodrigo? I looked at him. He avoided my gaze.

"Ugh!"

The pointy end of my heel pierced Gilther's shoulder. *I wanted it to hit his forehead.*

"Get the direction of the wind right next time."

Rodrigo looked at me as if he didn't know what I was talking about. I ignored him and walked over to Gilther. Then I took hold of my shoe embedded in his shoulder and wrenched it out. His shoulder began to bleed.

"You crazy b—"

Gilther tried to grab my hair. However, Rodrigo, who was suddenly next to us, grabbed his wrist forcefully.

"You... you..."

"Sorry, my foot is slippery. I'll be more careful from now on." I smiled elegantly and put my shoe back on.

"If you dry madman's grass along with March leaves and the fall root of beggar's grass and mix it, you can make a potent sleeping pill."

"Why would I ever use that?"

The poison-making teacher, whose face was covered in a black hood, glanced at Gilther.

"I am simply telling you the recipe. How you use it is up to you."

He was right. A strong sleeping drug was extremely useful. There were plenty of things you could do once your target was asleep.

Gilther pouted and shook his head. The teacher ignored him and returned to his concoction. He added a powder made from the mentioned ingredients to water and boiled it.

"As you can see, this has no scent, no color, and no taste."

"Do you die if you drink a lot of it?" Gilther interrupted the teacher once again.

"Gilther!" Roa shouted.

Gilther flicked her forehead as he said, "How dare you interrupt me while I'm talking?"

Roa put her hands over her forehead. Her eyes were glistening with unshed tears. Billian's face flushed red. He was clearly angry, but he didn't say anything to Gilther.

"I'm sorry," I exclaimed, rubbing my forehead. *My family is such a mess.*

"This is very different from how your siblings treat you."

"We're a bit special."

Rodrigo nodded as if he had figured something out.

"Why are you making that face?" I asked him.

"Because I understand why you get along so well with your siblings."

"And why is that?"

"Because it is impossible not to love you."

Seriously? I gave Rodrigo's thigh a sharp slap under the table. Rodrigo didn't so much as wince and turned back to listen to our teacher. I was the only one unable to concentrate because my heart was fluttering so much.

"Before the next class, you must make this sleeping pill yourself, use it, and write a report on the results."

The lesson was boring. It was mostly about things I already knew. Finally, the teacher gave us an assignment and was about to end the lesson when Gilther's hand shot up.

"Will you, teacher, take responsibility if something bad happens because of this drug?"

Why does he keep glancing at me?

"Count Kartina will take responsibility. If the intention behind it was purely to complete the assignment, of course."

"All right, that's fine."

What's fine? Is he planning on putting pills in my food?

Nathaniel stood amidst the flowers and vibrant greenery with gardening shears in hand. However, the more he snipped, the worse the flowering tree looked. The sorcerer Pagolas approached carefully, not to step on any of the countless blossoms littering the ground. Once he stood close enough to Nathaniel, he bowed his head.

"You summoned me, Your Holiness?"

Nathaniel slowly turned toward him and looked at him. He handed the sorcerer a flower he had just cut.

"Thank you, Your Holiness."

Pagolas reached out a hand for the flower, but Nathaniel let go of it just before his hand was in place, dropping the flower onto the ground. Pagolas froze, his hand in mid-air.

"There are people..."

Nathaniel turned away again and continued to cut the tree. The sound of the shears neatly severing branch after branch sent chills down Pagolas's spine.

"People who expect a reward despite doing nothing. Naive people who expect there to be no strings attached to a gift."

"I... see."

"I despise such clueless people."

Pagolas pulled his hand back and lowered himself to his knees.

"Your Holiness, please give me another chance."

"What are you doing, Pagolas? You're making it look like I am scolding you. Get up. The ground is cold. Your knees are already in bad shape."

Just as Nathaniel had said, Pagolas's knees were in bad shape. Because Nathaniel had stabbed a sword into his knees. That was already three years ago. Whenever Nathaniel said the word "knee," Pagolas remembered that day. That shameful, horrifying day.

"No, Your Holiness. I am simply finding my place as someone much lower than you. Please do not pay me any mind."

"If you insist, I will not stop you."

Nathaniel put down his gardening shears, finally satisfied, and sat in a nearby chair.

"I hear the Veloki Kingdom matter has imploded."

"Blanche has betrayed us."

"What did I tell you? Do not trust anyone."

What followed were words that no one would expect from the pope, known for being more merciful than any pope before him.

"Did you get rid of him?"

"Well..." Pagolas was sure that the pope already knew the answer, but he couldn't say that.

"You are taking care of things at the western border, are you not?"

"Of course, Your Holiness. We are using the financial support you sent to experiment—"

"Ha! Pagolas! Who sent what?"

"I misspoke, Your Holiness!"

Realizing Nathaniel was furious, Pagolas pressed his forehead against the cold ground. Nathaniel's sharp gaze seemed to stab into the back of Pagolas's bowed head. Pagolas was a powerful sorcerer. His monstrous creations made Nathaniel happy. However, they weren't particularly bright, which Nathaniel was not happy about.

"Soon, I will be holding a prayer meeting for the starving citizens by the western border."

"Yes, Your Holiness."

"Sir Erhart will be there as well, so it would be good for you to familiarize yourself with him there."

"Yes, Your Holiness."

Nathaniel stood. The sound of his robes trailing against the ground faded into the distance. Pagolas only straightened up after the sound was completely gone. He hurriedly left.

An encounter with Erhart. He knew that his life would be forfeit if he failed this time. He needed to be well prepared, but time was running out.